CW00732516

OTHER BOOKS BY $

The Trident Security Omega Team Series

Mountain of Evil: TS Omega Team Prequel

A Dead Man's Pulse: TS Omega Team Book 1

Forty Days & One Knight: Book 2—Coming Soon

Summer's Fall: Book 3—Coming Soon

The Doms of The Covenant Series

Double Down & Dirty: Book 1

Entertaining Distraction: Book 2

Hammered & Nailed—Coming Soon

The Blackhawk Security Series

Tuff Enough: Book 1

The Malone Brothers Series

Take the Money and Run: Book 1

The Devil's Spare Change: Book 2

The Ultimate Price: Book 3—Coming Soon

The Hazard Falls Series

Don't Fight It: Book 1

Stand Alone Novels

The Road to Solace

Scattered Moments in Time: A Collection of Short Stories & More

THE BID ON LOVE SERIES (WITH 7 OTHER AUTHORS!)

Going, Going, Gone: Book 2

THE COLLECTIVE: SEASON TWO (WITH 7 OTHER AUTHORS!)

Angst: Book 7

SPECIAL PROJECTS

The Trident Security Coloring Book

Word Search For Warriors: Authors For a Cause
Word Search for Warriors: Volume II

Shaded with Love Volume 5: Coloring Book for a Cause
Cooking with Love: Shaded with Love Volume 6

First Chapters: Foreplay Volume One
First Chapters: Foreplay Volume Two
First Chapters: Foreplay Volume Three

ANGST

A Novel

SAMANTHA A. COLE

Suspenseful Seduction Publishing

Angst
Copyright © 2018 by Samantha A. Cole
All rights reserved.

This copy is intended for the original purchaser of this book ONLY.
No part of this book may be reproduced, scanned, transmitted, or
distributed in any printed, mechanical, or electronic form without
prior written permission from Samantha A. Cole except in the case
of brief quotations embodied in critical articles or reviews. This
book is licensed for your personal enjoyment only. Please do not
participate in or encourage piracy of copyrighted materials in
violation of the author's rights. This book may not be re-sold or
given away to other people. If you would like to share this book with
another person, please purchase an additional copy for each person
you share it with. If you are reading this book and did not purchase
it, or it was not purchased for your use only, then you should return
it to the seller and purchase your own copy. Thank you for
respecting the author's work.

Editor: Eve Arroyo
Cover Artist: Judi Perkins of Concierge Literary Designs
Interior Design/Formatting: Samantha A. Cole

Published in the United States of America
This is a work of fiction. While reference might be made to actual
historical events or existing locations, the names, characters,
businesses, places, and incidents are either the product of the
author's imagination or are used fictitiously, and any resemblance to
actual persons, living or dead, business establishments, events, or
locales is entirely coincidental.

ISBN: 978-1-948822-32-9

AUTHOR'S NOTE

The story within these pages is completely fictional but the concepts of BDSM are real. If you do choose to participate in the BDSM lifestyle, please research it carefully and take all precautions to protect yourself. Fiction is based on real life but real life is *not* based on fiction. Remember—Safe, Sane and Consensual!

Any information regarding persons or places has been used with creative literary license so there may be discrepancies between fiction and reality. The missions and personal qualities of members of the military and law enforcement within have been created to enhance the story and, again, may be exaggerated and not coincide with reality.

The author has full respect for the members of the United States military and the varied members of law enforcement and thanks them for their continuing service to making this country as safe and free as possible.

Angst was previously published as part of The Collective Season Two but can be read as a standalone.

The Collective is a crossover collaboration by:

Riley Edwards, Ellie Masters, Erin Trejo, J.L. Leslie, Samantha A. Cole, Jade Royal Leona Windwalker, and B.R. Bradley

This book is dedicated to our readers. Without you, The Collective wouldn't be what it's become. The Collective Season Two authors thank you for reading our stories, joining our excitement with this collaboration, and for supporting our dreams.

CHAPTER ONE

"I swear, Nick, I'm almost to the point of putting some Diprivan into his bottle of Jack Daniels, and then, when he passes out, I'll tie him to the bed until he freaking tells me what the hell's going on." If anyone knew how frustrated Carson Matthews was, it would be his friend Nick Sawyer, a retired Navy SEAL. The two of them had hit it off after meeting at a club one night in San Diego, with their significant others, a little over eighteen months ago. Since then, Nick and Jake Donovan had moved to Tampa, Florida, after Nick opted out of the Navy, and Carson and Quinn Alexander had relocated to San Francisco, but they'd all stayed in touch. Nick and Jake had gone through a rocky start to their relationship, and much of it had been because Jake had been holding in a lot of his past, refusing to talk about it. But once he'd learned to let it out and go, their love for each other had bloomed.

"What's that?"

Carson switched his cell phone to the other ear, so he could pull his key ring from the front pocket of his surf shorts. "Diprivan? It's another name for Propofol—the anesthetic drug Michael Jackson overdosed on."

"Ah. Well, dude, the only thing wrong with that scenario, beside the fact it's probably illegal—even though you're an anesthesiologist—is that I'm pretty sure drugging and shackling your Dom to a bed is frowned upon in the lifestyle."

Snorting, he unlocked his and Quinn's assigned mailbox amongst the row of them by the curb outside their condo. "Pretty sure, nothing. I'm certain it is, but I'm running out of ideas. Something's bothering him. I know he's under a lot of stress lately and being a US Marshal isn't like it is in the movies—although Tommie Lee Jones did make being a bad-ass marshal look like fun. Anyway, between the move and one of his witnesses being killed on his watch, Quinn's just not himself lately."

"Wait, what? The one from a few weeks ago? I thought that was an accident."

After pulling out a bunch of envelopes, Carson locked the box again and strolled back up the walkway to his unit. "It was an accident—head-on collision. The old guy in the other car had a fatal heart attack at the wheel and crossed the double yellow line. His wife survived but was critical for a few days. Quinn's witness was just in the wrong place

2

at the wrong time. But it'd been only a week after he'd moved her. He's going through the 'what if' guilts. You know, 'what if I'd chosen a different town or city for her to live in, then she wouldn't have been driving down that road at that exact moment.'"

"Yeah, I know that 'what if' game all too well—it sucks."

Carson stopped in his tracks, his phone sandwiched between his ear and shoulder. While they'd been talking, he'd been shuffling through the mail when a red envelope caught his eye. In typed lettering, it was address to *Mr. Quinn Alexander and carson matthews*. Anyone else looking at it would have assumed the lack of capital first letters in his name had been a typo or something, but that, combined with the return address he recognized, had his heart rate picking up and his dick twitching in his shorts. "Hey, Nick, hang on a second. I think I've got an answer to my problem."

Carson tore open the envelope, pulled the contents out, and scanned the letterhead and text. A smile spread across his face as he grabbed the phone again. "Hey, we just got an acceptance letter to The Cellars! We're invited to a meet and greet on Friday, if we can make it, but regardless, we're officially members. Freakin' awesome! Thank your cousin for helping to get our application fast-tracked. Some club play is exactly what I need to get into Quinn's head."

The Cellars was an exclusive BDSM club in Napa Valley that had a waiting list to get in. Nick's older

3

brothers, Devon and Ian, and their cousin, Mitch, owned a similar club in Tampa. When the Sawyers had opened The Covenant several years ago, they'd started a network for BDSM club owners and managers throughout the United States for sharing information on banned members, new types of play, and other stuff. Mitch had met Damien Stackhouse and Derek LeMark at a lifestyle convention a while back and had called in a favor to the Dominants. Quinn and Carson had still needed to be fully vetted, but their names had been moved to the top of the list.

"That's great. I'll tell Mitch you said thanks. Listen, I've got to get going, but the reason I called you in the first place is to tell you Jake and I are getting married a week from Saturday. It'll just be a small ceremony and reception on a party boat in the Gulf off Clearwater Beach. I know it's last minute, but in the private security business we can't plan too far ahead. In fact, we've got our fingers crossed nothing critical pops up between now and then. Anyway, we want to invite you both but will understand if you can't make it."

"Congratulations!" he said before groaning. "Yeah, I honestly don't think we can swing it, Nick, but if we can manage it, somehow, we'll be there. I'll check my schedule at the hospital tomorrow, and have Quinn see if he can take some time off. I'll get back to you in the next few days."

"Sounds good. And good luck with Quinn. Just

remember, drugging and shackling is not exactly a bright idea—but I can give you some pointers on the shackling if you run out of alternatives."

Letting himself back into the condo, Carson chuckled. "Great. Talk to you soon."

"Ciao, buddy."

Several hours later, staring at the ceiling in the darkened bedroom he shared with Quinn, Carson tried to force his body to relax and his mind to go blank, so he could get some sleep. It was just after midnight, Quinn wasn't home yet, and Carson was due at the hospital at 6:00 a.m. Three months after taking the position of Chief of Anesthesia and Perioperative Care at San Francisco General Hospital and Trauma Center, he was finally starting to get comfortable among his colleagues and staff, although he knew there were a few people he'd never win over. He hadn't been the only one surprised when the board of directors went outside the hospital to find their new chief when the former one had passed away suddenly of a heart attack. After eight years on the staff at UC San Diego Health-UC San Diego Medical Center, Carson had mailed in his resume, with no expectations of being chosen. While his record was spotless and his credentials exceptional, he'd assumed the board would promote from within the hospital's ranks. But lo and behold, he'd gotten the call . . . and then the job.

The first problem he'd faced was telling Quinn, because Carson had never even told him he'd applied for the position. That'd been a difficult conversation since Carson wasn't supposed to keep anything from his Dom. A huge part of their relationship was about openness and honesty, and he'd skirted around both. That wasn't the only reason Quinn had been pissed when he'd heard the news. The other was that in order for Carson to take the position, Quinn had needed to request a transfer with the US Marshals where he worked in their Witness Security Program —the public commonly called it the Witness Protection Program, thanks to movies and television. It hadn't been an easy thing to do since Quinn oversaw making sure dozens of people, who'd needed to start their lives over under assumed identities, were safe from their pasts.

In fact, that was what Quinn was doing out so late tonight—taking someone into protective custody and shipping him or her out of the area for safekeeping. At least, that's what Carson thought Quinn was doing. A sliver of worry that his Dom had lied and was cheating on him fluttered into Carson's brain, but he shoved it back out again. Just because he'd been in relationships before that had failed because his other half had cheated on him didn't mean it was happening again with Quinn. His lover had never given him a reason to doubt anything he said or did, but once burned, twice shy, and in Carson's case, it was times two—twice burned, four times shy.

In the silent condo, Carson heard the front door open then close, followed by the heavy footsteps he'd come to recognize as Quinn's. He breathed a sigh of relief. It wasn't always easy being in love with someone in law enforcement. In fact, one needed the patience of a saint, understanding, a thick skin, and an ego that wasn't the size of an elephant. Carson had to remind himself that, although Quinn loved him, there were many times the marshal's work had to come first in their relationship. Lives were at stake. The same could be said for Carson's career. There'd been days when their plans had to be canceled because of mass-casualty incidents that had the hospital's OR hopping with surgical patients lining the halls and filling the emergency room.

Quinn slowly made his way through the condo, stopping in the kitchen, the living room, the spare bedroom that had been turned into a shared office, and then finally the master bedroom. Using the sliver of moonlight coming through the blinds, Carson watched as his lover kicked off his shoes, then stripped down to his boxer briefs. Carson's breath hitched when Quinn strode into the attached bath. He'd never get tired of seeing the man's sculpted body. From his strong arms, carved shoulders and back, tight ass, and lean, muscular legs, the man was freaking sin on two feet. And his front was just as magnificent as his rear.

The toilet flushed, followed by water briefly running in the sink, before Quinn returned to the bedroom. From the far side of the bed, Carson pulled the covers down for his Dom.

"Thanks," Quinn said, his usually strong, rumbling voice sounding tired, as he climbed into bed and got comfortable on his back.

"Everything go okay tonight?"

Lifting his arm, Quinn silently ordered Carson to scoot closer to his side. There was no way Carson was going to refuse his Dom—this was the first time in several days they were in bed and awake at the same time. Sometimes it sucked they both had careers that could have whacky hours. It wasn't uncommon for Carson and his staff of anesthesiologists to be called in for multiple emergency surgeries in the middle of the night. He laid his head on Quinn's shoulder, wrapping an arm across his chest. Inhaling deeply, he was still able to detect a faint trace of the Dolce & Gabbana Light Blue aftershave his lover had put on hours earlier. Carson had given it to him on his last birthday, along with the matching cologne.

"Yeah," Quinn finally responded. "Things got delayed with the local cops, though. Apparently, they jumped the gun and called us in, then decided they weren't done interviewing the witness." He turned his head and yawned loudly. "Sorry. By the time they were done, we got stuck in rush-hour traffic on the way to the safe-house."

The deputy never referred to a witness by gender, nor would he ever give any hint of where he and his partner had transported them. It'd taken Quinn a few months of dating Carson before fessing up that he didn't just have a desk job with the federal agency, as he'd originally told him, which Carson had suspected had been a half-truth. Quinn had said he'd learned to keep that intel to himself until he was certain a relationship had staying power. Even now, though, there was very little he could or would talk about, and it was always in generalizations. It wasn't that he didn't trust Carson to tell him anything to do with his job, but his witnesses' lives where in his hands. Having his lover kidnapped and tortured by someone desperate enough to do it to find the person who was supposed to testify against them wasn't a chance Quinn could take, no matter how slim. And Carson fully understood it. He had relatives in law enforcement, so it wasn't a foreign subject to him.

A few moments of silence passed, before Carson spoke again. There were several things he wanted to tell Quinn before the man fell asleep. "Nick called me today. He and Jake are getting married on a yacht in the Gulf near Clearwater a week from this coming Saturday—just family and close friends. They're hoping we can make it but understand if it's too short a notice."

"I doubt I can get enough time off to fly out and back."

"That's what I told him. Maybe in a few months we can take a trip and meet them in Key West." Carson and Quinn had gone there two years ago and loved it. They'd talked about going back again someday, but, now that Carson thought about it, neither had mentioned it in a long while.

"Yeah, maybe."

Carson bit his bottom lip at the indifference he heard in those two words. He counted to ten in his head before bringing up the next bit of news. "We got a letter in the mail today."

"Hmm? From who?"

"The Cellars—our application was approved. We're invited to a meet and greet on Friday."

His heart sank when Quinn let out a heavy sigh. "I don't know if I'm up to going on Friday. It's not required, is it?"

"No, it's not." Swallowing hard, he added, "But, Sir, I need this . . . you need this . . . *we* need this." He lifted his gaze to Quinn's face. "Please." Carson hated the desperation in his voice, but he was running out of options. If they didn't fix whatever was wrong in their relationship, things were going to go downhill. The last thing he wanted was to lose Quinn. He was madly in love with his Dom and couldn't imagine a life without him.

After a moment's hesitation, Quinn turned his head and kissed Carson's forehead. "If it means that much to you, babe, then we'll go."

Carson knew it was only a partial victory, but it was a start. Now he just had to figure out how to win the gold.

CHAPTER TWO

"Hey, what are you in the mood for? Chinese, pizza, or subs?"

With irritation, Quinn looked up from the pile of paperwork spread out before him. His partner, forty-four-year-old Bryan Owens, was waving a bunch of takeout menus he kept stored in the top drawer of his desk, and Quinn grimaced. "Anything that doesn't give me more heartburn than I already have. Don't you have any menus from a place with food that's not covered in grease or preservatives?"

Tossing his pen down, he pulled open the drawer to his right and grabbed the bottle of antacids he'd picked up last week. He frowned when he realized it was more than half empty already. Popping three of the chew-tabs in his mouth, he tossed the bottle back into the drawer and shut it with more force than needed.

Owens selected one of the menus and dropped

the others on his desk. The dark-skinned man was in pretty good shape for someone who ate takeout more than anything, although it wouldn't be a surprise if his cholesterol levels were sky high. He refused to tell anyone after he'd found out the other marshals had been taking bets on what it was after their last annual physicals. "Subs it is, since you can get rabbit food from here."

Glancing at the name of the chosen deli on the back of the paper the other man was studying, Quinn picked up his pen again, then rattled off his order. "Roasted turkey, avocado, and sprouts in a sun-dried tomato wrap, with a side of summer slaw."

After his choice was recorded on a Post-it note, he went back to his paperwork. He had to finish up the weekly reports, using codes so the entries couldn't be traced back to a specific witness. Grabbing another file from the stack on his desk, he opened it and silently cursed. Sophie Carroll, aka Susan Elliot, a thirty-three-year-old woman who would never see her thirty-fourth birthday. She'd been killed in a car accident a few weeks ago after Quinn had relocated her following her testimony against members of a cult. She'd once been a part of Children of Destiny until she'd witnessed the psychotic leader and two of his cronies commit cold-blooded murder. After she'd escaped the compound and contacted the authorities, she'd been placed in federal protective custody since the perpetrators had crossed state lines to cover up their crime. Ironically, she hadn't been killed by any of the leader's zealous followers who'd threatened her. She simply happened to be in the wrong place at the wrong time. As a result, Quinn couldn't stop the "what-if" scenarios that popped up in his mind whenever he thought of her. What if he'd placed her somewhere else? What if he'd insisted she get the available apartment two blocks away from the one she'd chosen? What if he'd arranged for her to get a bigger vehicle that would have given her more protection from the Cadillac that had broadsided her after the elderly driver had suffered a heart attack?

It'd been the first time he'd lost a witness based on the decisions he'd made and it was eating him up inside even though everyone had said it wasn't his fault. Accidents happen, but he couldn't get rid of the feelings of guilt and remorse that plagued him. Never had one of his personal witness been located by the person or people who'd wanted them dead. In fact, since the start of the Witness Security Program in 1971, no witness following the program guidelines had been harmed or killed while under the active protection of the USMS. In the fourteen years Quinn had been a marshal, the only witness deaths in his case files, prior to this, had been due to illness or old age.

Rushing through the file, he signed the bottom of the page and then put the folder in the stack that would be going to the records department. Needing some air, he stood and addressed his partner. "Call in the order, and I'll go pick it up."

Raising an eyebrow, Owens stared at Quinn a moment. In the short time the two had been partners, Owens had proven he was an astute man—picking up the different moods and emotions of those around him that others missed. Whatever he saw had him not questioning the curt command. Instead, he nodded. "Sure. Thanks."

Quinn grabbed his sports coat and pulled it on to cover his gun holster and shield. He strode out the door without another word. The overcast skies were still holding back the forecasted showers he'd heard about that morning on the radio, so he decided to walk the four blocks to the sub shop. It would give him time to clear his mind.

After dodging the pedestrian traffic for two blocks, his mind shifted from Sophie Carroll to the other person who'd been plaguing his thoughts in a negative fashion lately—not that it was Carson's fault. Quinn knew he hadn't been the best Dom in the world to his submissive lover over the past few months, but the funk he was in had been taking over all aspects of his life. Ideally, he should sit down and talk things over with Carson, but the anesthesiologist had his own shit to deal with settling into his new position at the hospital. For now, it was best for Quinn to keep things to himself until he had everything squared in his mind before dumping it all on Carson. The job was getting to him, something he hadn't realized until recently. When he'd first joined the Marshals after leaving the Marines, he'd been stoked—it'd been his dream job. But now? Now it was starting to take a toll on both his mind and body. Case in point, his esophagus was still on fire, despite the antacids. Maybe he should make an appointment with his doctor and see if there was anything else he could take for it.

Rubbing his sternum in a failed attempt to make the burning go away, he crossed the last intersection and headed into Sal's Sub Shop. Even though Owens had called in the order, Quinn still had to stand in line to pick it up. The place was popular and usually crowded no matter what time of day it was. Getting in line behind two uniformed EMTs on a lunch break, Quinn glanced at a stack of newspapers nearby. It was the same old crap in the headlines. He was convinced most of the hot-button issues escalating into violence lately was due to the press stirring up shit. Sensationalism sells, and if a story wasn't loud enough to make the daily quota of sales, then a few twisted words were inserted to fire up the masses.

The sound of something plastic hitting the floor brought his attention back from the news. He glanced down and saw a pen at his feet. Reaching down, he snatched it up and held it out to the female EMT in front of him, before she could bend and get it. "Here."

Her smile was a little more than friendly as she stared at him. It was a response to his appearance he was more than used to. Not that he was vain, but over the years, he'd drawn in more than his fair share of appreciative looks from both men and women. Although, he'd never been attracted to the latter. He'd known since puberty he was gay but had hidden the fact from his high school football and baseball teammates. He'd lost his virginity at fifteen to a gay neighbor, three years his senior. It wasn't until he'd left the Marines during the whole "don't ask, don't tell" era that he'd come out to his family and friends. While some had been surprised, others had told him they'd suspected he was gay for years. But while he hadn't come out in the military, that didn't mean he'd been celibate during his time there—far from it. Through another gay Marine, he'd found the BDSM lifestyle and joined a semi-private club about forty-five minutes from his base. It hadn't taken him long to discover a respected club in San Diego where he'd been assigned after joining the Marshals. That was where he'd met the submissive Carson. The two had danced around each other for a few months, as Carson had been in a contracted relationship with another Dom until it had eventually gone south. Approaching another Dom's collared submissive was a big no-no in the lifestyle. But once Quinn had found out the hot-looking sub had been uncollared, he'd made a beeline for him at the first opportunity and negotiated a contract with an open-end date. Four years and several amended contracts later, they were still together.

"Thanks," replied the woman, whose nametag on her shirt read "Jen Galloway—Paramedic."

If Quinn had been attracted to women, he might have flirted back—she was definitely pretty—but not wanting to encourage her, he pointed behind her, indicating the line had moved. "You're welcome, and I think you're up."

He didn't miss the disappointment in her eyes, but her smile didn't falter as she turned back around and joined her male partner giving his order to one of the sandwich makers. When it was Quinn's turn, he rattled off that he was picking up an order, under his surname, ready to say "Owens" in case the other man had used his when calling it in.

Just as the paramedics were getting their lunches handed to them, the radios on their hips squawked to life, announcing "shots fired, multiple injuries" at a park about fifteen blocks away. The male medic cursed and threw a $20 bill on the counter while the female grabbed the sack containing their sandwiches and drinks. Dodging people walking into the shop, the two ran out the door. Once again, Quinn was glad he'd gone federal instead of taking the police exam somewhere. At least when he dealt with people at a critical time in their lives it tended to be in a controlled environment. He'd never been a fan of blood.

Ten minutes later, Quinn was back at his desk, about to dig into his lunch, when his supervisor's door swung open and Supervisory Deputy Margaret Muldoon stuck her head out, eyeing who was at their desks and who wasn't. "Owens, Alexander, Brighton, and Szymanski. Head over to the federal courthouse. A credible bomb threat was called in, and a suspicious package is on site. They need all the help they can get to cover the judges and prisoners."

Dropping his sandwich onto the thick, white paper it'd been wrapped in, Quinn yanked open his desk drawer and grabbed three more antacids. His day just went to total shit.

THROWING HIS MASK AND GLOVES IN THE designated bin, Carson picked up the patient's chart and followed as the assistant surgeon and two nurses moved the sixteen-year-old girl, who just had her appendix removed, to the recovery room. She was very lucky since it'd been hours away from bursting. The surgeon was on his way to talk to her parents and give them an update.

Plucking his favorite pen from the pocket of his scrub shirt, Carson took a seat at the recovery room desk and finished the paperwork on the patient. He glanced at the clock on the wall and saw he was already on an hour of overtime. Not that his department head position garnered time and a half. At least that was his last surgery. It'd been a busy day between the scheduled surgeries, several emergencies, and the baby boom that seemed to be happening on the maternity ward. His team of anesthesiologists had been hopping from one case to the next, doing what they did best. He'd been quite impressed with the surgical staff at the hospital. His predecessor had done a good job, but there still had been a few ideas Carson had implemented using tactics he'd learned in medical school and on the job in San Diego.

"Dr. Matthews?"

"Hmm?" Carson turned his attention to the OR's head nurse standing a few feet away as she set the telephone back on the cradle. "What's up, Helen?"

"There's been a code red called for the ER. Multiple shooting victims. At least three en-route with a four- or five-minute E.T.A."

Crap. So much for calling it a day. "All right. I'll head down there. Who else is free?" he asked, standing and handing her the finished chart.

"Dr. Marchetti just went into the locker room. I'll let him know. And Dr. Ballard's surgery is just finishing up."

"Good. Send John down. I'll let you know if we need Kay." He glanced at the dry erase board on the wall with the list of the anesthesiologists and anesthetists. Two more of them were still in surgery and would be there for a while. Two others had already finished up for the day but hadn't signed out too long ago. "Page JJ and Patty and put them on standby in case we need them to come back in."

"You got it. Rooms one, two, five, and nine are clean and ready to go. Six is being cleaned now. Let me know if we're going to need more than that."

Carson had already been walking backward

toward the double doors leading to the hallway and elevators. Once Helen was finished giving him and update, he spun around and hit the square, silver button on the wall that made the automatic doors open. Noting both elevators were on upper floors, he veered toward the stairs. Jogging down the steps, he took his stethoscope from around his neck to keep it from bouncing off his shoulders during his three-flight trek. Striding down the hallway past staff rooms, the ER's X-ray room, bathrooms, and more, he stepped out of the way of a nurse pushing a young woman in a wheelchair. What caught him off guard was the patient was wearing a city EMS uniform, with a white sheet laid over her lap. She was clutching her abdomen as tears rolled down her cheeks, and he saw blood starting to seep through the thin cotton covering her lower body. Carson raised an eyebrow at the ER nurse who shook her head and mouthed the word "miscarriage" to him as she hurried past, evidently on the way to the maternity and GYN floor. Grimacing, but knowing the gynecology staff wouldn't need his help unless the young woman required surgery, he continued down the hall.

The emergency room was still bustling—in fact, it appeared even busier than earlier and that didn't include the patients in the ambulances pulling up to the bay outside. The three trauma rooms, each with two cubicles, were ready for them as the medics and EMTs unloaded the stretchers from the back of the rigs. San Francisco General had the city's only Level-1 Trauma Center, so the most critical patients would be brought there. If the victim count was high, triage would be done at the scene to determine which ones could go to other hospitals.

The first victim, who was already in a trauma room as the others were being rushed in, was a middle-aged, Hispanic woman with IVs in both arms, an oxygen mask on her pale face, and a bloody trauma dressing over her abdomen. *Shit.* Belly wounds could be anywhere from simple to completely fucked up, depending on the size of bullet, angle of entry, and a host of other factors.

The next two victims brought in were male and seemed more stable—one with a gunshot to the thigh and the other had been hit in the shoulder.

Carson listened as the EMS personnel rattled off the injury details and vital signs to the ER staff as each victim was transferred from the ambulance gurneys to the trauma room beds. Moving to the head of the injured woman, Carson saw she was losing consciousness from the blood loss. He pointed to a nearby instrument tray. "Nurse, let me have the intubation set."

As the ER physician examined the belly wound, he barked out orders for blood work, type and cross-matching for a transfusion, X-rays, and more. Meanwhile, Carson grabbed an ambu-bag and hyperventilated the patient, so he could put a breathing tube down her throat. As soon as the preliminaries were done, she'd be heading for surgery. Speaking of which, the surgeon on call, Lillian Coats, hurried in.

Eyeing the controlled chaos in three cubicles of the trauma room, her gaze shot to the male medic who'd brought the belly wound in. "Are there any more coming?"

The tall man shook his head as he helped the nurses cut off the rest of the victim's clothing. "No. There was a little girl that didn't make. Shot in the head. Nothing we could do for her."

Frowns appeared around the room, but no one stopped working. Horrible deaths weren't uncommon in a city the size of San Francisco, and the trauma center saw far more than its fair share of tragedies, but it didn't mean the staff was immune to the senseless killing of a child. Carson knew it hadn't been an easy decision for the medics to pronounce the little girl dead, instead of working on her. If there'd been even the slightest chance she could have survived, she would have been the first patient to arrive. He could only image what the bullet had done to her head to have EMS leave her at the scene.

Twenty minutes later, Carson took ten seconds to shoot off a text to Quinn, letting him know duty called and he'd be late getting home, before following the belly wound patient into OR #2. So much for the couple's early dinner plans before going to the club. Carson couldn't care less about the meal, but he'd really been looking forward to going to the club again tonight. They hadn't played during the meet and greet at The Cellars the other night but had made love when they'd arrived home. However, they'd both been so hot for each other by that time, after observing some incredibly erotic demo scenes at the club, that conversation had been the last thing on Carson's mind. Maybe he was afraid of what Quinn would say when he was called out about the fact that things were far from good between them. It was the only reason Carson hadn't brought the topic up yet. But, soon, he had to do it, and whatever the response was he'd deal with it. He just hoped the relationship wasn't beyond repair.

CHAPTER THREE

Pulling into the parking lot of Turk's apartment building, Carson stopped behind a moving van with several men starting to unload it. He'd met Simon "Turk" Turkawitz at the surfing beach they both enjoyed after Carson and Quinn had moved to San Francisco. Turk and Carson had hit it off right away, even though Turk was straight, and the men had only a few things in common interest-wise. Their only similarities, besides a love for surfing, were being fans of most professional sports and having sarcastic wits.

Turk was what he, himself, called a mutt. People were always shocked when they got to know him because he wasn't what he appeared to be—a defensive tackle for the Niners. He stood six feet six and weight about 260, but despite his size he was an extremely agile surfer. Half Hawaiian, half Polish, his dirty-blond hair was in direct contrast to his charcoal eyes and dark skin. His aw-shucks, good-old-boy attitude also didn't match with the fact he held a Master's in fine arts. To top it all off, he was one of the most sought-after jewelry designers in California and probably beyond. It wasn't uncommon for his unique pieces to be wrapped around the necks, wrists, or fingers of the latest Emmy, Academy, Grammy, and Golden Globe nominees on the red carpet. He often joked people expected him to be stealing jewelry, instead of designing it.

Last night, Turk had called Carson, asking for a lift to the beach this morning, after his SUV had been towed for a shot alternator. The two had hit the surf early, and, as it always did, riding the waves had helped Carson relax and clear his mind. It was the only activity other than a BDSM scene that let him give himself over to something or someone taking control. The ocean could be a sadistic Dominatrix at times, and all Carson had to do was let instinct take over to stay balanced and upright. Everything else got pushed from his mind—work, the problems with Quinn, the turmoil bubbling to the surface in the city they lived in after that little girl was shot and killed the other day, and other issues plaguing him.

Putting the Chevy Suburban in park, Carson hit the tailgate release button, so Turk could retrieve his board. The big man held up a fist. "Thanks, dude. 'Preciate the lift."

Carson bumped the other man's knuckles with his own. "No problem. It was a great morning."

"Yeah, except for that wipeout I had." Turk opened the passenger door and gingerly got out. His hip where his surfboard had smacked him, after it had flipped out from under him, had already started to turn black and blue before they'd left the beach, and Carson knew it was going to get worse.

"Ice that and get the Arnica on it before it gets too stiff."

"Got it, Nurse Ratched."

Carson chuckled as his phone rang. "That's Dr. Ratched, asswipe."

The passenger door slammed shut, and Turk gave him a friendly but sarcastic middle finger before going to the back of the vehicle to grab his board. Snatching the cell phone from its cradle attached to the dashboard, Carson answered the call. "Hey, Mom. What's up?"

"Oh, hi. I was expecting it to go to voice mail. I figured you'd still be out surfing. Didn't you go?"

Relaxing back into the driver's seat, Carson watched the moving men work as he spoke to his mother. "Yup. I went early though. Everything okay? She rarely called this early in the morning."

"Yes. Well . . . not really. I guess you haven't heard yet." He sat up a little straighter, worried about what she was about to say. "Danny White was killed in a car accident last night. I thought you'd want to know."

Surprised, but relieved the bad news hadn't hit closer to home, Carson relaxed again. A bigoted bully,

White had never been one of Caron's favorite people in high school. Dislike had morphed into abhorrence when he came out of the closet in college and brought his boyfriend home at Thanksgiving during his senior year. His family had known about his sexual preference for a few years, but at his request, they'd kept it to themselves until he'd worked up the courage to go public. Bringing Shawn home had been his coming out moment in his hometown. While most of his friends back in Savannah, Georgia, had been supportive, Carson and Shawn had been subject to White's homophobic rant when the man had run into them at a bar with other people from high school. Carson would have decked the bastard if it hadn't been for several friends getting between the two adversaries and the bouncers interfering and throwing the loud-mouth out of the place. There had been no love lost between the two men, but Carson's mother didn't know that.

"Sorry to hear that." In a way he was since White's twin sister, Jaclyn, had been the complete opposite of her brother. Carson occasionally chatted with her on Facebook, not that he was on it often with work and all.

"I'll sign your name and Quinn's to the flower arrangement I'm sending to the funeral home." Carson almost laughed out loud at the irony but managed to keep it inside. A sardonic grin still spread across his face, though, as his mother continued. "The funeral plans haven't been announced yet, obviously, since it just happened last night. That poor family."

"Mm-hmm." After glancing down at the middle console, Carson rolled his eyes. *Damn idiot.* Turk had left his wallet sitting there. As his mother droned on with some other local news he had no interest in about people he barely remembered, he swung his SUV into a parking spot, turned off the ignition, grabbed the wallet, and got out. When his mother took a breath, he jumped in. "Mom, I gotta run. Can I call you back later?"

"Oh, sure, honey. Give Quinn a kiss for me. I'll talk to you whenever. Love you."

"Love you, too, Mom. Bye."

Striding across the parking lot, he passed the moving truck and the men. A well-dressed, Asian man was barking out orders, and Carson figured he was the owner of the stuff. As he approached the lobby entrance of the building, Carson saw the weight of the door push the rock that had been placed to hold it open. It began to close on one of the moving men who was carrying two large boxes, which seemed more bulky than heavy. The top one rocked, as the door struck the man's arms, and Carson lunged forward to catch it.

"Shit! Oh, crap. Thanks, dude," the young man said, clearly relieved the box hadn't hit the ground. He took the final steps into the lobby. "You can just put it back on top."

"What floor you going to?" he asked, holding the

oversized box. "I've got to go up anyway—I'll give you a hand."

"The top floor. Thanks."

"No problem." Turk was on the same floor, so Carson didn't mind helping the guy out.

The guard manning the front desk was on the phone and must have assumed Carson was one of the moving men because he didn't stop him from walking past. The high-end building was filled with luxurious apartments, and the lobby was elegantly decorated. Carson had been in his Turk's apartment several times before. The last time had been about two weeks ago, with Quinn, Turk's brother and his boyfriend, and Turk's girlfriend, Leesa, to watch a Lakers/Kings basketball game. Surprisingly, it'd been the only woman in the room who'd known more NBA stats than anyone else.

Carson hit the "Up" button when they reached the elevators. When the doors slid open, they stepped inside the car and rode to the top floor in silence. When they stopped and the doors opened again, Carson followed the other man out as he turned left. At the far end of the hall, an apartment door was open and an Asian man was waiting for them. Actually, a gorgeous Asian man was waiting. Carson was madly in love with Quinn, but he'd have to be dead not to appreciate the hottie before him. He was shorter than Carson's five-ten by a couple of inches, and his slim body was lean and muscular. Long, jet-black hair had been pulled back into a ponytail, which, when he turned to the side, Carson could see hung down to his waist. The man was by about five or six years younger than Carson, maybe even more, but he had a dominant presence to him that was clear even from this distance. Gay or straight, he brought out a natural, submissive reaction from Carson whose gaze immediately and involuntarily dropped to the floor.

"Hisoka Tsukuda?" the moving guy called out.

"Yes, that's me," the hottie answered as they approached, his bass voice fit the commanding aura he exuded. "Just let me get the door for you." He held it open for them as they entered the apartment.

"Thanks. These are labeled clothes. Where do you want them?" The man pointed to an open bedroom door, and Carson followed his temporary employer who added, "They're bringing your sofa next."

"Okay, great."

Carson and the other guy deposited the boxes against a wall in the bedroom. The unmade bed was in sharp contrast to the way everything else in the room had been precisely placed.

Exiting the room again, he found the unit owner still standing near the door, waiting. "Thanks for doing this. I really appreciate it."

It sounded like he thought they were doing him a favor and not a job. Carson's eyes met his, but the dominance there had his gaze involuntarily dropping to the floor again. "No problem, dude." Whenever he'd been hanging around Turk, his dumb-blond, surfer lingo, as Quinn jokingly called it, came out. He pulled Turk's wallet out of his jeans pocket. "My buddy left this in my car, and I was just bringing it up to him. I was just helping out on my way up."

"You aren't with my father's group?"

The older man downstairs must be the father. Carson shook his head. "Nope. I work at the hospital. Since it's my day off, I went to catch some waves with Turk. He lives at the other end of hall." Trying to rid himself of the submissiveness he felt in this man's presence and bring things back to an even level, he grinned. "I'm an anesthesiologist at San Francisco General. Name's Carson Matthews."

"I'm Hisoka, and thank you," he replied.

"Don't worry about it." Carson shook the man's extended hand, before letting go and heading for the door with the moving guy on his heels. "I'm sure you'll see me around and have an opportunity to repay the favor."

Leaving the moving guy waiting for an elevator, Carson continued past, on his way to Turk's apartment. He hoped Hisoka hadn't thought he was flirting with him—well, in a way, he had been, but that was Carson's personality. He'd seen a bit of interest in the other man's eyes and had reacted to it. It wasn't as if he'd ever cheat on Quinn, but it was a nice shot to his ego to know he could still garner appreciative looks from another man. And as soon as that thought hit him, his smile vanished. He didn't want another man's appreciation—he wanted Quinn's. But they were back to being roommates passing each other in the hall again. Carson had been putting in long hours at the hospital, and for the past few days, Quinn had been working late hours on a protection detail he couldn't talk about. Hopefully, that would end soon so they could get some time in at the club. Carson wanted to ask Quinn if they could bring Carson's cousin Danilo, who was also a submissive in the lifestyle, as a guest one night.

Danilo's father, Ricardo, was the half-brother of Enzo, Carson's father, making the two younger men cousins. Enzo Mateus's American-born mother had divorced his Brazilian father and returned to the United States with their son. When he was old enough, Enzo anglicized his surname to Matthews, so his son and nephew had different last names, despite their common ancestry. But that wasn't the only difference between the two. Whereas Danilo was six feet two, with dark brown hair and green eyes, Carson stood five ten, with his dirty-blond hair and startling blue eyes. Both men were in excellent shape —Carson through surfing, and Danilo through yoga.

Five years older than his cousin, Carson had taken him under his wing when he'd moved to Sacramento a few years ago to attend college. While it was several hours away from San Diego, the older man had still kept an eye on Danilo, visiting him and inviting him down the coast whenever possible. Shortly after Carson and Quinn had moved to San Francisco, the younger man had also relocated there, where he worked as a musical therapist for Bayside Health Groove. His career took him into hospitals, long-term care facilities, and hospices, where he worked with patients suffering from a variety of illnesses and injuries. Carson had found his cousin's form of therapy fascinating and had consulted Danilo when he'd made music available in each operating room to help soothe the patients.

Making a decision to convince Quinn a trip to the club was in order as soon as possible, Carson knocked on Turk's door. The man's small, mixed-breed dog started yapping from inside the apartment. Grinning, Carson got ready to greet Trixibelle and give Turk some shit about all the things he could've bought with the man's platinum American Express.

CHAPTER FOUR

The heavy bass music pulsated through the air as Quinn led Carson and Danilo around the club. Carson was wearing his black, leather collar that told the other Doms he was taken, while his cousin's neck was bare. It wasn't uncommon for Danilo to accompany them to a BDSM club, but this was his first time at The Cellars. He'd expressed interest in checking the place out after learning Quinn and Carson were now members. They had been allowed to bring a guest after the person was vetted. Members valued their privacy, and security was tight as a result. Quinn knew Nick Sawyer's brothers and cousin ran their club in Tampa the same way. Every member and guest were investigated before being allowed to step foot in the place.

Dressed in his black leather pants and boots, topped off with a burgundy, button-down shirt with the sleeves rolled up to his elbows, Quinn felt the stares of men and women who were drawn to his dominant presence. Other gazes were concentrated on the two submissives he was with. While cousins, Carson and Danilo were like night and day in their skin tone, hair and eye color, and height, each incredibly handsome in his own right.

Having done his best to push all thoughts of work from his mind, Quinn greeted several Doms he'd met at the meet and greet, and another subsequent visit to the club, while introducing himself, Carson, and Danilo to others. It was amazing to watch the change in Carson upon entering a club. Out in the real world, he was easy-going, boisterous, and able to charm anyone he met no matter the age or gender. At home, with just Quinn around, he was a lot more mellow and relaxed, as if he didn't need to impress anyone. At the club, though, was where Carson's true self really shined. He was able to leave all stress and problems at the door, something Quinn was never able to completely do unless in the middle of a scene when rational thought was thrown to the wayside, instinct and need dominating. Here in the club, Carson's submissiveness was loud and clear—he didn't need to take charge like his job demanded, nor did he need to be Quinn's equal, as they were at home—for the most part. He willingly handed over all decisions to his Dom and just felt at peace. When they'd first started dating, they'd discussed what they both got out of the lifestyle, and Carson had been the most articulate sub Quinn had ever been with. Carson's good looks, intelligence, personality, and hot-damn physique all combined into one yummy package, and more than once had Quinn's jealousy rearing its ugly head when another man flirted with his lover. Thankfully, he had the willpower not to react with a throat punch on the few occasions it could have been warranted. Quinn didn't take kindly to men who touched Carson without permission . . . but then again, neither did Carson, though, he was usually able to dissuade the poacher from doing it again before his Dom could get involved. At least, in here, most, if not all, Doms would never cross the line of approaching a sub that was collared.

While Quinn engaged in a conversation with two unattached Doms, Carson and Danilo stood on either side of him, heads bowed in respect, hands behind their backs, clasping their forearms. Both were shirtless and shoeless, dressed only in leather pants and wrist cuffs. If Quinn was standing, and not in the middle of a scene, he preferred his sub to also be standing. Other Doms required their subs to kneel at their feet, but Quinn had always found it annoying. At six feet four, five inches taller than Carson, Quinn would either have to shout or squat down for his submissive to hear him over the din of conversations, scenes, and music.

The two men Quinn had been talking to stepped

away and were replaced by the club owners, Damian Stackhouse and Derek LeMark, and a small crowd of submissives. LeMark extended his hand first. "Master Quinn. Nice to see you this evening. I hope you and your submissives are enjoying yourselves."

The corners of Quinn's mouth ticked upward in a grin as he accepted the man's hand. "Not yet, since we've just gotten here, but the night's still young." He then held out his hand to Stackhouse, who took it in his firm grip for a brief moment before releasing it.

While LeMark was in a monogamous relationship with his submissive, Sally, who was tucked in close to his side, Stackhouse was another story. The man had two male slaves, one of whom was a switch—submissive to Master Damien, yet dominant to the others in the relationship—and three submissive females, all readily involved in a polyamorous arrangement. Quinn had no idea how Stackhouse kept them all happy but to each his own. Only two of the female subs were with him at the moment, but Quinn couldn't remember their names off the top of his head.

The Cellars was a magnificent place. The estate was on a large, Napa Valley vineyard, which concealed the fact there was a BDSM club in its midst. The dungeon was located below the main house, but the high-class decor was warm and inviting despite being underground. A ten-foot ceiling told how far into the earth the builders had had to dig before laying the foundation. Massive pillars held up the mansion above. Open-space play areas were offset by comfortable seating sections. Near where they were standing, a stage was set for public demonstrations. If a Dom wanted a semblance of privacy for a scene, see-through curtains could be pulled into place. Now, the sheers were tied to either side of the stage. A St. Andrew's cross had been pushed back, leaving plenty of room for a scene to take place in the space.

Standing on the stage, examining yards of Shibari rope sitting on a table, was an attractive Asian man. As Quinn watched, the man glanced up as if sensing someone's gaze on him. It was clear he was a Dom, not only from his state of dress—leather trousers that laced up the sides and a crisp, white, silk button-down with pewter buttons—but the way he carried himself. His waist-length, straight, black hair flowed freely. He nodded at Quinn, but then his gaze roamed over Carson and a flash of recognition in the man's eyes confused Quinn. He'd never seen the other Dom before, and couldn't imagine where he would know Carson from.

Striding across the stage, the Dom jumped down to the club floor and joined the three others and their subs. Stackhouse took care of the introductions. "Master Hisoka Tsukuda, I'd like you to meet another new member, Master Quinn Alexander." The two men shook hands. "And this is his submissive, Carson, and their guest, Danilo."

It didn't startle Quinn that Stackhouse was able

to rattle off the names of the club members as if each person was wearing a name tag. The man seemed to have a photographic memory, which Quinn had noticed on his prior visits. Nor was it strange he didn't include the submissives' last names. Here, in the lifestyle, they weren't expected to have a surname, especially if they were collared. What was surprising was the smirk that appeared on Hisoka's handsome face.

"Yes. Carson and I have met." At Quinn's raised eyebrow, the man explained, "Nothing to worry about, Master Quinn. I've moved into the same building as his friend, Turk, and Carson was nice enough to help the moving men bring up one of my boxes the other day. Interesting man, that Turk . . . a paradox, actually."

Muscles he hadn't realized had tensed relaxed as Quinn chuckled. "Definitely a paradox, but a nice guy."

"Yes, he is." While Hisoka had spoken to Quinn, his gaze had shifted to Danilo, and there was no disguising the blatant interest on the Dom's face.

Quinn had often acted as a negotiator for Danilo and Doms who wanted to scene with the submissive. When Danilo first started in the lifestyle, they'd agreed Quinn would be a mediator because of the fact he was able to filter out the bad Doms—those in the lifestyle for all the wrong reasons—easier than the sub could. But before Quinn could say anything, Hisoka returned his attention back to him. "Carson is also a bit of a paradox. A surfer, a doctor, a moving man, and now a sub—intriguing. He must keep you on your toes."

A small smile appeared on Carson's face, but he didn't say a word. Quinn hadn't given him permission to take part in the conversation, and the sub had been in the lifestyle long enough that he knew there'd be consequences if he did. "That he does."

Hisoka's again studied Danilo. "Master Quinn, I'm in need of a subject for my Shibari demonstration this evening. Is your guest available to be of service?"

Quinn pivoted slightly to his left. "Eyes up, Danilo." Carson's younger cousin obeyed the directive, and his gaze rose and slammed into Hisoka's. Quinn didn't miss the returned interest the sub was aiming at the Dom. "You heard Master Hisoka's question. Please answer him."

Danilo gulped as if he had a large lump in his throat, then licked his lips before answering. "I'd be honored, Sir."

Turning back to Hisoka, Quinn said, "Looks like you have a sub for the evening. I usually negotiate for Danilo if your interest goes beyond the demonstration."

The other Dom nodded. "Understood. Thank you, Master Quinn. Danilo, please go up on the stage, present, and wait for me."

"Yes, Sir."

After bowing his head in respect to the other Doms, Danilo did as he'd been told. Climbing the three stairs to the stage, he strode over to where the table of ropes had been set up and resumed the presenting position he'd been in moments earlier, but this time on his knees. The entire time, Hisoka's gaze had followed him. Once the sub was settled, the Dom returned his attention to the small group. "Master Quinn, I assume you'll be watching the demonstration."

"Even if it didn't involve Danilo, I enjoy watching Shibari scenes. I look forward to seeing your technique."

"Well, I hope you enjoy it then." With a nod toward the club owners, Hisoka excused himself with a simple, "Gentlemen," before joining his temporary sub on the stage.

Quinn spoke with LeMark and Stackhouse for a few more minutes, then led Carson over to a seating area in front of the stage. As the Dom sat in a leather chair, his sub knelt on a pillow beside him. Quinn studied him with a frown. Carson's gaze was on the floor, which was normal in this setting, but Quinn couldn't help but sense something was different . . . off. Carson had been quiet throughout dinner—well, that hadn't exactly been his fault since Quinn had been on the phone with work-related stuff for most of it. He'd wanted to make sure everything was squared away with one of his witnesses, before they came to the club tonight. Being in law enforcement, he'd received permission from LeMark and Stackhouse to carry his cell phone on his hip for emergencies. And if Carson was needed at the hospital, instead of Quinn carrying both phones, they just forwarded Carson's calls to his Dom's number. Otherwise, Quinn wasn't allowed to use his phone, and he had to answer all calls and texts outside the club. It didn't happen often, but there had been occasions over the past few years when they'd needed to cut short an evening of play.

Reaching over, Quinn cupped Carson's chin, gently forcing him to look up. "Are you okay, babe?"

"Yes, Sir."

Quinn's eyes narrowed. There had been no emotion in those two flatly-spoken words—nothing that would help him figure out what might be wrong. Before he could ask another question though, the overhead lights flickered, indicating the demonstration was about to start. An in-depth conversation would have to wait as the seats around them filled up with those interested in watching the show. Quinn had reserved a playroom when they'd first arrived, and they had about forty-five minutes before it was available. Relaxing back in the chair, he ran his hand down the back of Carson's head several times, then focused his attention on the stage as the exhibition began.

After reaching into his pocket and fishing out a small, leather thong he used to bind his hair back, away from his face, Hisoka picked up a microphone headset from the table. Once he was ready, he nodded at Derek LeMark who stepped onto the stage and clapped his hands loudly. Someone turned off the music for him. "Now that I have everyone's attention, I'd like to welcome you to tonight's demonstrations. I hope our invited guests find these informative and enjoy their peek into our playrooms. And, of course, if you're thirsty, there's always the bar. Just a reminder, though, after visiting the bar, you won't be allowed to play in a private room until either myself or Master Damian are satisfied you're sober. This is strictly enforced. Anyone trying to circumvent this will find themselves out the door, flat on their ass, with a permanent ban. Now, if you'll turn your attention to Master Hisoka beside me, he's got something he'd like to show you." Derek gestured toward Hisoka with a sweep of his arm, then bowed off the stage.

Hisoka took center stage, his voice reverberating through the overhead speakers. "Hello, everyone." The crowd turned their full attention to him. "I'm Hisoka Tsukuda, and like the other two Masters on tonight's program, I'll be doing a demonstration for you. My specialty is Shibari, so we're going to have some fun with bits of string."

Quinn chuckled along with several other people sitting in front of the stage. Hisoka went on to describe the types of ropes that could be used and some safety issues, before starting to wrap the rope around Danilo in an intricate design he called "The Gunslinger." Danilo eased into subspace as he was bound and by the time Hisoka suspended him above the stage, the submissive was "rope-drunk." His body had responded to being tied up by releasing endorphins that flooded Danilo's system, causing him to feel and act as if he'd had several, strong alcoholic drinks.

Several Doms had moved closer to the stage to get a better look at the knots and the design. After answering a few questions, Hisoka showed them how to safely lower the submissive before unwrapping the ropes from Danilo, who was still enjoying the subspace he was in.

At the end of the demonstration, Hisoka gave a brief bow of his head. "Thank you for coming. Now, please excuse me while I tend to the needs of my sub." Removing his headset, he gently guided Danilo to a chaise lounge that had been set up on the stage for him, then urged him to lay down.

Seeing that Danilo was in good hands and getting the necessary aftercare, Quinn checked his watch and saw that the playroom he'd reserved should be ready. One of the submissive attendants who cleaned the rooms after each scheduled scene would have brought Quinn's toy bag to the room for him. Standing, he held out his hand to help Carson get to his feet, before leading him toward the hallway where the playrooms were located. He hadn't thought about what scene to do tonight with his sub, and took a moment to give it some consideration. It'd been a while since he'd used a violet wand on Carson, so maybe he'd do that. Stopping at their assigned room,

Quinn took a deep breath and tried to get into the dominant zone he'd need for the scene, then turned the knob and opened the door. With a hand gesture, he let Carson proceed him into the room, then followed and shut the door.

CHAPTER FIVE

C arson silently followed Quinn toward the private playrooms. He was trying to keep his anger and frustration tamped down, but it was getting harder and harder to do. Several times over the past week, he'd tried to talk to Quinn about whatever was bothering him, but something or someone had interrupted them each time. A few times it had been Quinn's job, other times it'd been Carson's.

Then there was last night when Quinn had had to intercede in a fight in the condo next to them. Their neighbor had moved in a few weeks ago, and while Carson had been making dinner, her ex-fiancé had shown up, pounding on her door, threatening her. When Quinn had stepped outside to intervene, the drunken bastard had pulled a knife on the US Marshal—not a bright thing to do. Before Carson even realized that Quinn had left the apartment, the confrontation was pretty much over, with the asshole pinned to the ground, his wrist that had been holding the knife was broken, and the cops were on the way, courtesy of the woman's 9-1-1 call. Three hours later, after a trip to the police station to give his statement, Quinn was eating the dinner Carson had reheated for him. After that, Quinn had taken a shower and fallen asleep within minutes.

Even when Carson had managed to start a conversation, any time he'd tried to turn it into a serious discussion, Quinn blew him off somehow. And each time, it had dug deeper into Carson's gut. Then, right before the demonstration had started, Quinn had had the gall to ask if Carson was okay? Yeah, that was the straw that broke the camel's back. Either they were going to talk when they got into the playroom or Carson was going to explode. He couldn't take it anymore. The relationship between the two of them no longer felt like they were lovers, instead, it felt like they were roommates who occasionally had sex—nothing more. If he'd known the move to San Francisco would eventually drive them apart, he never would have taken the department head position.

Stopping next to one of the playroom doors, Quinn turned the knob, pushed the door open, then motioned for Carson to proceed him into the room. When the door closed behind them, the music volume dropped dramatically, although they could still feel the pulsating bass through the wooden door and floor. Glancing around the room, Carson took inventory of his surroundings. The outer wall was comprised of exposed, stone blocks, while the interior, wallpapered walls had been insulated to keep the sound levels down. Heated coils ran between the easy-to-clean, dark, tiled flooring and the cement foundation; the members could walk barefoot without being chilled. Rich golds and burgundies with hints of green brought the main club decor into the room. However, it didn't take away from the wrought iron racks of torture implements and shackles embedded in the stone wall, or the large St. Andrew's cross that stood in a corner.

"Stand next to the cross," Quinn instructed.

Carson had heard the directive, but he couldn't make his feet move in that direction. A feeling he couldn't describe other than desperation came over him, and his hands clenched. He couldn't do this. He couldn't play like nothing was wrong, yet he was so afraid to confront Quinn. If the end of their relationship was near, he didn't want to know, but he also couldn't act like nothing was wrong anymore, hoping it would fix itself.

"Carson?" Quinn stopped whatever he was doing and stepped in front of Carson, his gaze roaming his lover's face in confusion. "Babe, what's wrong?"

Biting his upper lip, Carson shook his head slowly. He couldn't look Quinn in the eye, his gaze pinned to the cleft in his chin, knowing he'd fall apart if he did.

He swallowed hard, then whispered the one word he never thought he'd have to say to his Dom, "Red."

Quinn's eyes widened. "What?"

Carson blinked away a few tears that were threatening to fall, then raised his voice a little louder. "Red, Sir. I—I can't do this. I—I can't . . . please, take me home."

Bringing his hands up, Quinn cupped Carson's jaw and held him in place. "Look at me. Damn it, Carson, look at me! What's wrong?"

"P-Please, just take me home. I—I can't do this anymore."

"Do what?" When Carson didn't answer him, Quinn stepped closer, his tone filled with bewilderment and shock. "Do what, baby? Are—Are you asking me to remove your collar? Is that it? You —You want out of our contract? Our relationship?"

Carson's watery gaze met his lover's. "I—I don't want that at all, but you're not leaving me any choice."

"What? Jesus, Carson, tell me what the fuck is wrong. What are you talking about?"

"Not here. Please. Can we go home and talk? Please."

He half expected Quinn to continue to demand Carson spit it out then and there, but after several seconds ticked by, the Dom dropped his hands and took a step backward. As if a curtain had fallen, Quinn's expression became impossible to read—

blank and unemotional—and that scared Carson more than he would admit.

Quinn gave him a curt nod. "Fine. Go to the locker room and get our things. I'll see if Danilo is ready to leave or if I have to arrange a ride home for him."

Without waiting for an answer, Quinn skirted around Carson and stormed out the door.

CONFUSION, ANGER, AND ANGUISH FOUGHT FOR supremacy in Quinn's mind as he strode out to the main room of the club. He had no idea what the hell was wrong with Carson, but it was clear the best course of action was to take him home then demand to know what had brought this all on. *Does he really want out? God, I hope not.* If Carson told him it was all over, Quinn didn't know what he'd do. As if his professional life being in turmoil wasn't enough, this would tear him apart.

Scanning the crowd, he spotted Hisoka sitting in a chair next to the chaise lounge where Danilo was still recovering from the subspace he'd obtained during their scene. Before approaching them, Quinn stepped over to where LeMark was talking to several people. "Master Derek, I'm sorry to interrupt, but may I have a word, please?"

"Sure," the club owner responded, before

addressing the small group he was with. "I'll be back in a moment."

Before joining Quinn a few feet away, he glanced at his submissive resting on a pillow on the floor nearby and made sure she was aware of where he was going. LeMark raised an eyebrow at Quinn. "Something wrong?"

"No . . . no, but Carson and I need to leave—work related," he lied. "Before I ask Hisoka, I wanted to make sure it was safe for Danilo to get a ride home from him, if he agrees. Danilo's still in subspace, so he needs to be monitored, whether I drive him home or Hisoka does."

LeMark nodded. "Understood. But Hisoka wouldn't be here unless he'd been fully vetted, just as you were. Would I trust him with my sub? No, but I don't trust anyone with my sub. Would I trust him with any other sub here? Yes. He was highly respected in the clubs he'd put down as references. Not a single negative word about him."

"Thanks. That's all I wanted to know."

"No worries. And I hope everything is okay with you and your sub." The Dom's concerned tone of voice said he wasn't fooled by Quinn's little white lie.

He sighed heavily. "So do I. Thanks."

Moments later, Quinn stopped in front of Hisoka, and the other man stood, his dark eyes narrowing. "Everything okay?"

What? Do I have a fucking sign on my forehead that says

my life is going down the tubes? "Yeah, just need to take my sub home. He's not feeling well. I was wondering if you wouldn't mind driving Danilo home when he's ready. He only lives about ten minutes from you."

Hisoka raised an eyebrow. "You made sure it was safe to ask me that." It wasn't a question but a stated fact. "LeMark or Stackhouse must have said yes." He didn't appear to be offended. In fact, his expression was one of respect.

"Yes and yes."

"As long as Danilo agrees, it would be an honor to drive him home."

Squatting down next to Carson's cousin, Quinn lightly shook the sub's arm. "Danilo."

"Hmm?" The young man was still enjoying the "rope-drunk" sensation.

"Open your eyes and look at me."

Danilo's eyelids fluttered several times before lifting all the way. "Yes, Sir?"

"Are you okay with Master Hisoka driving you home? Carson isn't feeling well."

The sub's gaze flittered from Quinn to Hisoka, who had taken his seat again. The heat that flashed in Danilo's eyes gave Quinn his answer before the sub spoke. "Yes, Sir. I'm very okay with that. Thank you, Master Hisoka."

The other Dom smiled. "You're very welcome, Danilo."

Yup. The two were definitely interested in each other. It'd been a while since Danilo had been in a collared relationship, and, hopefully, this worked out for him. But for now, Quinn had his own relationship to deal with . . . that is, if it still existed.

CLOSING THE CONDO DOOR BEHIND THEM, QUINN set his toy bag in the hall closet. "Go put on something comfortable, then have a seat on the couch."

Without a word, Carson nodded then headed for their bedroom. Shaking his head, Quinn entered the kitchen and retrieved two lowball glasses from a cabinet and a bottle of cognac from the bottom of the pantry. His mind flashed to the bar Carson had shown him in a magazine a few months ago that he wanted to have in their home one day. They'd been talking about buying a house together at some point, but they'd gone from a condo in San Diego to another one here in San Francisco. They just hadn't had time to research and look for a house, but that didn't mean Quinn didn't think they wouldn't have done it eventually. Now, he didn't know if it would happen at all.

From there, his thoughts went to the ring he'd wanted to have designed for Carson when he asked his sub to marry him. Again, he'd thought that was in their future. Quinn had been planning on proposing once he figured out what he was going to do about his job. Was he going to stay or find something else?

Would it even matter after tonight? Not if Carson was leaving him it wouldn't.

After pouring two ounces in each glass, he returned the bottle to the pantry, then carried the drinks into the living room. With his head down, Carson came out of the bedroom, dressed in his favorite sweatpants and a comfortable T-shirt. Quinn handed him one of the tumblers. "Here. Sit. I'll be right back out. Let me get changed, and then we'll talk. Okay?"

Carson still didn't look at him, but he accepted the glass. "Yeah. Okay."

Taking a deep breath, Quinn blew it out again, took a sip of cognac, then set his glass on the coffee table before retreating to the master bedroom. He was back minutes later, also having changed into a pair of sweats and a tee. Bending his knee, he sat down on the couch, sideways, facing Carson. He noted Carson hadn't touched the alcohol—the glass was on the end table beside him. Reaching over, Quinn grabbed his lover's hand, entwining their fingers, before resting them on Carson's thigh. "Why did you say your safeword?"

Still not looking at him, Carson replied, "Because I can't go through the motions anymore, wondering when you're going to tell me I'm not enough."

Quinn's eyes narrowed. "Not enough? Not enough what? What are you talking about, Carson? And, damn it, look at me."

Carson inhaled and exhaled three times before

turning his head. His troubled gaze slammed into Quinn's confused one. "I know you didn't want to move here, but I thought once we were settled in, you'd feel better about it. Then between my new job and yours, we didn't have as much time together, but, again, I thought it would get better. But ever since you lost that witness . . . you're just not here, Quinn. You won't talk about it . . . I mean, I know you can't talk about a lot of it, but you can tell me how you feel, and you won't even do that. I try to start conversations . . . not just 'what's for dinner' . . . but real conversations, and you blow me off. In the club, you're my Dom, but here . . . shit, here, you're my fucking roommate, and I can't live like that . . . I won't live like that. I'm sorry we ever left SD. If we hadn't come here, she wouldn't have been your witness, and you wouldn't feel responsible for her death. I can't change that, and I don't know how to fix this . . ." he used his other hand to indicate the metaphorical space between them ". . . canyon that's separating us."

Running his free hand down his face, Quinn swallowed the lump in his throat. He had no idea the stress he'd been going through had affected his relationship with Carson. He'd thought keeping everything to himself until he figured it all out had been best since Carson was dealing with everything to do with his new position. Damn it, he'd screwed everything up.

Quinn squeezed Carson's hand. "I . . . I'm so sorry,

babe. I had no idea I was messing things up between us. Please believe me when I say that was never my intention, nor was it to have you think it was because of you in any way, shape, or form. Because it wasn't." He scooted closer and ran his hand through Carson's blond hair, before resting it at his nape of his neck. "Oh, babe, I'm so sorry. Item number one on our contract is openness and honesty, and I blew that— big time. Yeah, her death hit me hard—it was the first time I'd ever lost a witness. And I know I've been playing the 'what if' game—"

"Bad things happen to good people . . ." Carson interrupted and shook his head. "We both know that and can't change it. You can't think you're God and everything bad that happens is your fault."

"I know. I get it, I do. But that's only half of it. I didn't realize it until after it happened that I'm . . . I'm burnt out. The job . . . I don't know if I can do it anymore. It's not just about my witness, it's everything. There are riots all over the place after that little girl was killed, everyone in law enforcement has a target on their back, the hours, the drop-everything-and-run emergencies, the stress . . . all of it. I've got heartburn that could kill a horse almost every day. At first, I thought it was the move —settling into a new office, dealing with new people, and getting to know my new partner and supervisor —but now I realize it's more than all that. I honestly don't think I can survive until my twenty years are in, but if I leave now, I'll only get a fraction of my pension unless I find something where I can transfer the time over. So that's another thing I'm stressed about. I'm so sorry I didn't tell you any of this before, and I had no idea it was affecting us. I just haven't been able to figure out what to do and, with all you have to deal with at the hospital, I thought I could solve it on my own, and then when I had all the facts, we'd sit down and talk."

Carson snorted. "Ya big dummy. What the hell do you think I'm here for if not to be your sounding board? Let me *help* you figure things out. I'm not just some gorgeous arm candy and a fantastic lay . . . I've got a fucking brain, remember? My diplomas are on the wall in the office, if you need a reminder. And, damn it, why didn't you tell me you were having stomach problems. I'm scheduling you for testing with someone from the gastroenterology department first opening they have. And then cardiology to make sure that's not an issue either." He stroked Quinn's cheek with his knuckles. "I love you, Quinn. Please remember I'm more than your sub. I'm your life partner, and partners are there for each other—for everything. Promise me you'll talk to me when something's bothering you, instead of pushing me away and trying to handle it on your own."

A sexy smile spread across Quinn's face, as the last of the tension that had tied him into knots back at the club finally left him. "I promise. We'll talk more tomorrow. Right now, I want to start filling in the distance I've created between us."

Tightening his hand on the back of Carson's neck, Quinn pulled him closer, his head descending until their mouths met. At first, the kiss was gentle. Quinn brushed his lips across Carson's, followed by a small lick with his tongue, urging his sub to open up and let him in. There was no resistance as Carson melted, trailing his hands up Quinn's arms, until they wrapped around his neck. Quinn moved closer, forcing his sub to lay flat on his back on the couch. There would be no kink this time—Carson didn't need that right now. What he did need was to know Quinn loved him. But just because things were going to be more vanilla didn't mean Quinn would ignore his dominant nature.

Leaving Carson's mouth, Quinn kissed his way down his lover's body, shoving Carson's shirt up his torso and his sweatpants down his legs until he was gloriously naked. Wrapping his hand around Carson's cock, Quinn slowly pumped him as he suckled the man's nipples. Carson moaned. His eyes fluttered shut, and he squirmed under the sensual ministrations. Moving lower, Quinn felt the taut abdominal muscles beneath his mouth quiver.

Going up on his knees, Quinn ripped his own shirt up and over his head and tossed it aside, then got rid of his sweatpants. Before returning to Carson, he reached into the drawer of the end table and pulled out the tube of lubricant that was kept there for times like this. With heavy lids, Carson followed his every move, his hands gripping the arm rest above his head, and his cock, long and proud, against his lower abdomen, twitching with need.

After putting some lube on two fingers, Quinn ordered, "Spread your legs and start jacking off. I'm going to make you cum before I fuck your ass, hard and deep."

"God, yes!" Carson set one foot on the floor and hooked the other on the back of the couch. Grasping his cock, he set a leisurely pace, pumping up and down, his gaze never leaving Quinn's as the Dom ran his two lubed fingers over his anus.

Pushing one finger, then both, past Carson's sphincter, Quinn thrust in and out, stimulating his prostate. Carson's back bowed, and his eyelids shut under the intense pleasure he was receiving. His hand tightened around his shaft and sped up. Using his free hand, Quinn cupped Carson's sac, rolling and tugging it.

"Fuck, Sir! That . . . oh, God! Please don't stop. That feels so . . . shit! So good!" The sub's breathing hastened. Most times he could stave off his orgasm, drawing out the scene, but it didn't look like this was one of them. And that was fine with his Dom.

Unable to resist the pre-cum he saw, Quinn leaned down and licked the tip of his cock, causing Carson to falter his hand job and his hips to buck.

As Carson's body prepared for its impending explosive orgasm, Quinn fucked his lover's ass faster with his fingers. "Cum for me, babe. That's it. Love watching you cum for me."

With a roar, Carson went over the edge. Streams of cum erupted from his cock onto his torso. While he was still coming, Quinn removed his fingers and replaced them with his rock-hard dick. As always, the intense pleasure he got when fucking Carson bareback was mind-blowing. They'd foregone condoms after the first six months of their relationship, and Quinn never wanted to go back to using them.

Spreading his knees wider, he forced Carson's legs further apart. Thrusting hard, Quinn somehow managed to keep his gaze on Carson, who was languishing in the afterglow of his climax. Caught between wanting to cum and wanting to fuck his lover's ass for hours, it wasn't long before Quinn no longer had a choice. His balls drew up into his body as streaks of lightening coursed through him. With a final, deep plunge, he spent himself inside Carson with such intensity, he almost passed out.

Moments later, still seated to the hilt in Carson's ass, Quinn leaned down for a kiss as both their breathing and heart rates returned to normal. "I love you, babe. I'm going to spend the rest of my life making the last few months up to you. Think you can handle that?"

"If it's anything like this—absolutely. And for the record, I love you too."

CHAPTER SIX

After putting his empty coffee mug into the dishwasher, Carson strode back into the dining area where Quinn was sitting at the table, having breakfast and jotting things down on a yellow legal pad. He was updating his resume, although he still had no idea where he was going to send it. There were plenty of private sector companies in the SF area that could use his training and experience, but he wanted to research them first before contacting them.

Placing his hand on Quinn's shoulder, Carson bent down and kissed him. "I've got to get to work. Do you want to try to go to Roka Akor tonight?" The popular restaurant on Montgomery Street was one of their favorite places to eat, with its sushi and steakhouse choices on the menu.

"Yeah. As long as nothing pops up between now and then." With the riots around the city getting bigger and more violent, either of them could end up having to work if emergencies arose. Quinn glanced at his watch. "Shit, I've got to hop in the shower." He stood and brushed his lips across Carson's. "I love you. I'll give you a call around lunch if I can, all right?"

Carson smiled. "It's been a while since you've done that."

Thinking about it for a moment, Quinn realized he was right. Quinn used to call Carson at least once a day to check in and just say hi. Sometimes he had to leave a voice mail because the anesthesiologist was in surgery, and other times Quinn only had time for a quick hello. However, there was rarely a day he didn't reach out to Carson at some point while at work, at least until several weeks ago. For a few days, he'd sent texts instead of calling because he'd had too much on his mind. He hadn't realized until now how much he'd unintentionally pulled away from Carson. "It's been a while since I've done a lot of things. I plan on making it all up to you."

"I'm looking forward to it."

Five hours later, Quinn was starting to feel better about looking for a new career. He'd sent out a few feeler emails to some contacts in the private sector, before getting elbow deep in a new case. The Dallas and Miami offices both had new witness that needed to be relocated after testifying at trials and getting death threats as a result. Quinn took the Miami case while Owens would take the Dallas one after he got back from the agency firearms range where he was requalifying on his job-issued weapon. They had to set up new identities for each person, and in the Dallas case a spouse, then find an ideal place for them to live in safety. There was a ton of paperwork that had to be done, in addition to researching available apartments for them to get settled in for at least the first few months.

As it had been since the protests and riots had started after that little girl had been shot and killed in the crossfire of a gang shootout, a flat-screen TV hanging on the wall in the bullpen of the marshal's office, was on. It was on the local news, so they could stay up to date with what was happening around the city. The national channels, like CNN and Fox News, were also reporting on the riots, but they would also switch over to other stations.

Glancing up, Quinn watched the red, "Breaking News" banner scrolling across the bottom of the screen, announcing the latest live update from one of the female beat reporters. From the looks of things, she was about a half a block away from another protest that was getting out of hand. The local station had switched over to its larger affiliate which broadcast across the states.

"The streets of the Sea Cliff area of San Francisco are beginning to look like a war zone as the National Guard has been called in. Another mob of angry citizens has gathered in support of the protesters who have surrounded City Hall and the Northern

District Police station where channel 9 news is told Police Chief Brown is in the building with his detail.

"So far, he's refused to comment on what began as a peaceful candlelight vigil for nine-year-old Holly Springs. The little girl was gunned down during what is being called a gang turf war . . ."

As the reporter droned on, Quinn's eyes shifted to the chaotic activity behind her. Police in riot gear were trying to push back the crowds. In the foreground, several people, who appeared to just want to get out of there, hurried past the camera, and . . . *Fuck!*

It couldn't be, he thought as he shot to his feet and moved closer to the TV to get a better look at the blonde woman who clearly had no idea she was on a nationally televised news broadcast as she stood on the street corner. But, damn it, that was her. Laura Barnett, aka Harper Russo, sister of incarcerated mobster Frankie Russo who'd put a $1 million price tag on her head after she'd squealed on him to the feds, was one of Quinn's witness—sort of. She'd been assigned to him during her initial relocation but had eventually opted out of the WITSEC program. No matter what Quinn had said, she'd refused to stay in —that didn't mean he hadn't helped her, of course. Using his underground contacts, he'd set her up with a new identity, and shown her how to stay off the grid so her brother's minions couldn't find her. For close to two years, she'd been successful, keeping Quinn in the loop when she moved or changed names again.

For some reason, she trusted him. It was by sheer coincidence they were in the same city now—she'd moved here several months before he and Carson had. While he hadn't gone to see her at the guest cottage she'd been renting or her job—not wanting to draw attention to her for any reason—he still knew where to find her.

Grabbing his lightweight jacket, he glanced around. Owens still wasn't back from the range yet, and everyone else was knee deep in their own cases. Since Laura/Harper wasn't in the program, Quinn didn't want to put her on anyone else's radar. He could handle this alone—besides, it'd been less than three minutes since her face had appeared on the screen. Even if she was recognized, it would be at least a few hours before any hitman dispatched could find her. *Damn it.*

On his way out the door, he let the office manager know he was checking on a witness—she didn't need to know which one or the fact that Harper wasn't sanctioned—then hurried out to his department-issued Crown Victoria. Peeling out of the parking lot, he tried to call Harper's cell phone, but after several rings, it went to voicemail. He disconnected the call without leaving a message, then redialed. Again, it went unanswered. *Shit, fuck, damn, and every other curse word out there! Pick up the fucking phone!*

It took him longer to get across town than usual. Some streets were blocked by the police trying to contain the riots and looting going on, while other streets were on the verge of gridlock with drivers who'd also been rerouted. The entire twenty minutes, he continued to call her number. Since it was midday, unless something had changed, Harper was most likely at the café where she'd been working for several months. If he didn't find her there, he'd head to her little cottage next.

Finding the street leading where he needed to go had been barricaded, Quinn flagged over one of the police officers and flashed his shield. He was then allowed to drive around the blue sawhorses and continue past. Pulling into the café's parking lot, he hadn't expected to see the café's front window completely shattered. A young man, probably a busboy, was knocking the remaining shards from the frame. Quinn scanned the area for anyone or anything else out of place. The riots were about two blocks away, so it didn't take him long to determine that no one stood out as a potential problem. Most likely, whoever had broken the window had been a rogue protestor who'd gotten around the cops. Parking his car, Quinn killed the engine and got out.

Opening the door to the café, he sighed in relief the moment he spotted Harper, surprisingly, in the ardent embrace of a tall, brown-haired man. *Shit.* He hoped it wasn't more than it looked like, because he was about to turn her life upside down once again. Love on the run rarely worked out for anyone.

He glanced around the place. There were only two customers and a few employees, talking about the punk who'd thrown a rock at the window and ran. Quinn's attention returned to Harper, who still wasn't aware of his presence. He tried to relax his facial features, to not to raise any alarms, then tried to get her attention. "Ahem. Laura?" While in his head, she would always be Harper, he'd been doing this long enough to remember to use her alias.

She froze in the other man's arms, then turned slowly and put some distance between them. It was then Quinn realized her hand was wrapped in a bloody towel. The guy frowned at the intrusion as Harper's eyes widened at the sight of Quinn standing before her. He had to get her out of here and somewhere safe. Raising an eyebrow, he asked, "A word?"

Her boyfriend's expression hardened, and he grasped Harper's upper arm and began to pull her behind him. Well, at least he was protective of her. "And you are?"

"My boyfriend," Harper blurted out before Quinn could speak.

Ah shit. Here we go again. It wasn't the first time he'd been thrown under the bus for the sake of someone's cover, but if the way the other man's body recoiled at the announcement and the thunderous look raging in his eyes were any indication, things were about to get ugly.

Somehow, Quinn managed to appear as if he hadn't been startled by her words. The jilted bastard wasn't so lucky. He looked ready to tear the place apart as he glared at both of them. Quinn kept his body relaxed, but he was ready for anything as the guy unleashed his angry words toward Harper. "You've been in my bed for the past nine months, and you have a man?"

Harper winced at his accusations and tried to cover her tracks. "It's, um, we have an open relationship. And I never made you any promises, Mac. The thing between us was nothing more than fun."

She was lying through her teeth, and Quinn wondered if her boyfriend realized it or was he too blinded by rage. When he locked eyes with Quinn, it was clear it was the latter. "Mac" nodded his head in disgust before turning and striding toward the double, swinging doors that probably led to the restrooms and back entrance of the café. "Good to know," he muttered as he shoved the doors open, slamming them against the walls.

Harper stared after him with longing for a few moments. Silence filled the room as the other employees looked on in confusion. Finally, Harper faced Quinn, sadness and regret filling her watery eyes, the tears hadn't yet spilled over. She swallowed the lump that had to be in her throat. "Ready?"

It was a scene he'd observed far too often. Living a lie to stay alive had to be one of the hardest things a person had to do. Quinn nodded and held the front door open for her. "Let's go."

She put a false smile on her face and waved

goodbye to her coworkers as if it was the end of her normal shift and she'd see them again tomorrow. But Quinn knew that wasn't going to happen. Her life here was over. He'd take her back to her little cottage to quickly retrieve what she could carry in a knapsack or duffel bag, then he'd stash her in a safe house while he hit up one of his contacts for new ID for her. Again, her not being in WITSEC forced him to work outside the system. One of the first things he'd done when he'd moved to San Francisco was make his own underground contacts—a forger, an arms dealer, and someone who could be trusted to run some not-so-legal errands for him, among other things.

Quinn followed her outside to the parking lot, the door closing behind him finalizing the last moment of her life here. Harper started walking to his right, but he grasped her upper arm and steered her toward his vehicle. "Get in."

She didn't say a word until they were pulling out of the parking lot. "What are you doing here?"

Unable to control a frustrated snort, his gaze shot to her before returning to the roadway in front of him. "I take it you have no idea your pretty face was plastered all over a national news broadcast about the riots less than an hour ago."

"What?"

Without even looking at her, he knew she'd paled at his announcement. He made a left turn before answering her. Even though he'd never been to her place, he knew where it was. "Yup. You walked by a reporter and cameraman doing a live broadcast. To top it off, you stopped on the curb for a few seconds before the light turned green. Seriously? The road was shut down. You didn't even notice there was no traffic and you could've danced ballet across the street without getting hit by a car. Damn it! I thought I taught you better, Harper." He glanced at her. "What the hell were you thinking? The only thing missing was a big fucking neon sign saying, 'Here I am, big brother, come and fucking get me.'"

"I—I'm sorry, Quinn. I had no idea."

"Obviously." Reaching under his seat, he grabbed the baseball cap he kept there and handed it to her. "Put that on and pull it low in the front. Keep your head down. I don't need your face showing up on any traffic cameras."

Once her face was hidden, he jutted his chin toward the bloody towel. "How bad's your hand? Do you need stitches?"

Harper shook her head. "Not too bad. Some asshole threw a garbage can through the window, and I got hit by a piece of flying glass."

He slowed, then stopped for a red light. His anger and frustration were ebbing. Harper hadn't ended up on TV on purpose. The last thing she'd do was put herself in danger. Now that Quinn had her, he'd help her disappear again. "Let me see."

"It's fine, really. A couple of butterfly bandages and it'll be fine. I already cleaned it out, and it doesn't feel like anything's still there. Where are we going?"

"Your place to pack your bags, and then a safehouse until I can get you a new ID and figure out where to send you." She was quiet for a few blocks, and Quinn took a deep breath and let it out before putting aside the last of his frustration. "What was that about back at the café?"

"What do you mean?"

He rolled his eyes at her. "Hello? Am I wearing a Mr. Oblivious name tag? C'mon, Harper. What's with the green-eyed monster you just blew off? That wasn't just some random guy trying to pick you up."

She shrugged. "It's over, so there's no need to explain. What are you doing in San Francisco?"

He snorted again, letting her know her change of subject was painfully obvious. "I transferred a few months ago after Carson accepted a position here." They'd chatted one day while he'd been training her to shoot the handgun he'd gotten her. While she knew he was gay and Carson was his longtime boyfriend, she didn't know the anesthesiologist's last name, what he did for a living, or where he worked. "The less contact I had with you the better, but I did manage to figure out where you worked and lived, and that's only because I taught you how to fly under the radar."

A block away from her cottage, he pulled into a chain pharmacy and parked as close to the door as he could. "Stay here and keep your head down and the doors locked."

"Where are you going?"

"To get you stuff for that cut. It's highly unlikely your brother saw you on the news, managed to get a phone call privilege, got ahold of one of his minions, who then got ahold of a hitman in San Francisco who was able to track you down in less than an hour. So, it's safe to assume I can run inside for three minutes and get what you need without getting you killed. Capisce?"

"You're not Italian." When all he did was raise an eyebrow at her, she sighed. "Capisce."

"Thank you. Now keep your pretty head down and stay put." Without waiting for her to say anything more, Quinn exited the vehicle and hurried into the pharmacy. Thanks to a little old lady in line arguing about the sale price of a tube of Preparation-H, it was more like five or six minutes before Quinn returned to the car and climbed in. After handing Harper the white bag filled with a bottle of peroxide, gauze pads, a roll of gauze wrap, and a package of butterfly bandages, he started the engine and pulled out of the parking lot.

Glancing at the clock on the dashboard, he did a mental tally of what he had to do over the next few hours. Get Harper's stuff, contact his forger, then get her to a safehouse for the night. By tomorrow morning, he'd have a destination for her and get her on her way. He hoped Carson hadn't been dead set on going to Roka Akor tonight, because dinner looked like it was going to be a delivered pizza. *Damn it.*

CHAPTER SEVEN

The ER and OR departments were jumping. Carson hoped the riots would die down soon because San Francisco General was a busy enough hospital without all the additional patients they were receiving who'd been injured by the unruly mobs or the police trying to control them. Somehow, he'd managed to catch Quinn's call before lunch. As of 11:00 a.m., they were still on for dinner at Roka Akor, but Carson knew that could change in a blink of an eye with a single phone call from the hospital or Quinn's office or one of his witness.

Carson had been pleasantly surprised when he'd come out of his second surgery around 10:00 a.m. and found Quinn had sent him a huge Edible Arrangements bouquet of chocolate-dipped strawberries and other fresh fruit—Carson's favorite. It had been Quinn's way of apologizing, again, for everything. The Head of Anesthesiology had been teased by some of the hopelessly-romantic nurses in the department, who'd wanted to know what the special occasion was or what Quinn had done that he was trying to make up for. Of course, Carson had kept the details to himself and told them he'd only share if they dropped the subject. Thankfully, they'd taken him up on the offer.

"Dr. Matthews?"

With the chart of his next patient in his hand, he turned back to the nurse's desk in the pre-op room. "Yes, Amanda?"

"It's Dr. Tao asking for you. He's down in the ER." The nurse held out the phone.

He thanked her as he accepted the handset from her. "Yeah, Steve, what's up?"

"The shit hit the fan again," the other anesthesiologist replied. "Got two stab-wound vics from the riots and a cop with massive head trauma. He got hit in the head with a baseball bat."

"Shit. All right. I'll look at the schedule and see who can take what. You want the cop?" Tao was the most experienced doctor on Carson's staff when it came to head trauma cases and brain surgeries.

"Yeah. As soon as his CT scan is done, we'll be up. Kiprovski's doing the surgery, and Adams will have one of the stab wounds. Not sure who's doing the other one yet."

"I'll let everyone know. See you in a bit."

Hanging up, he informed the staff that the emergencies would be up soon. Three routine surgeries would have to be delayed a few hours. Just when he thought everything was set, the Labor & Delivery department called and needed someone for an emergency C-section. Carson was ready to bang his head against the wall as he stared at the schedule on a large dry-erase board, trying to figure out who he could send. It was going to be a long afternoon. Hopefully, Quinn was having a better day than his lover was.

SON OF A FUCKING BITCH!

Quinn's heart pounded as fear coursed through him. The door to Harper's cottage had been kicked in. He pulled out his weapon and searched the three-room structure, coming up empty handed. Surprisingly, the place hadn't been ransacked, and, thankfully, there was no dead body or blood around. The window in her bedroom was open, and he hoped that meant she'd escaped before whoever was sent to kill her had gotten to her. And Quinn was certain there had been a hit ordered—this was no coincidence. If Frankie Russo couldn't participate in torturing his sister for turning him in to the feds, then he would want her killed outright. No fuss—just put a bullet in her head and be done with it.

Just to be safe, Quinn checked the area behind the cottage, making sure she wasn't lying in the dirt somewhere. After a few minutes of searching, he found footprints that had to be Harper's. They were small enough to be from a woman her size, and the distance between them and the lack of heel marks indicated she'd been running. The prints continued across the property behind the cottage and then disappeared onto the next street. On his way back to the cottage, Quinn noticed another set of footprints he'd missed. They were parallel to the first set, but these had been made by a man and the presence of heel marks meant the guy had been walking, probably tracking Harper's prints as Quinn had done. As far as the marshal could tell, she'd made it out of there. The problem was he had no idea where she was now.

Three hours. He'd been gone three hours, longer than he'd expected. While she'd been gathering her stuff, he'd gotten a call from the office. Another bomb threat had been called in to the federal courthouse, but this time, the suspicious package that had been found apparently was indeed an explosive device. Quinn hadn't wanted to leave Harper there, but she'd convinced him she'd be fine. After all, it'd only been less than ninety minutes at that point since she'd been on TV. Before Quinn had left for the courthouse, he'd told her to stay hidden and that he'd be back for her as soon as he could.

Stepping back into the cottage, he took inventory. Aside from the clothes in her bedroom, there weren't many personal items around. No photos, or pieces of memorabilia most people had lying around their homes. A search didn't turn up her gun, so hopefully she had that on her. He also couldn't find her stash of fake IDs. When he'd been teaching her how to disappear, he'd made sure she had at least two backup sets of identification and an emergency bundle of cash. So, one of three things could've happened, she had them with her; the hitman found them and took them; or, she'd hidden them so well, Quinn couldn't figure out where they were. His bet was on the first option. That would have been the first thing she'd retrieved. Everything but the gun, cash, and IDs were considered luxuries. He'd drilled that into her head many times.

Making sure there was nothing that would alert anyone to who had really been living there—he was sure the landlord would call the police after finding the door kicked in—Quinn left without leaving any of his own fingerprints behind. Harper's weren't on file anywhere, but his were, and the last thing he needed was the FBI or one of Frankie Russo's minions knocking on his and Carson's door.

After getting in his vehicle and pulling out of the driveway, Quinn called Harper's cell phone, not too surprised when it went to voicemail. The ringer had been muted earlier when he'd picked her up at the café. At the sound of the beep over his Bluetooth, he said, "Harper, it's Quinn. Call me and let me know where you are. I'll come get you." He rattled off his number even though he knew she had it memorized.

Quinn spent the next hour driving around, searching a six-block radius around her cottage, with no results. He left two more futile messages on her voicemail. Shaking his head, he tried to refocus. There were too many variables—Harper could have jumped on a bus or a trolley, taken a taxi or BART, hitchhiked, disappeared into the chaotic protests, or holed up somewhere out of view. Or she could have been caught by whomever had kicked in her door. "Damn it!"

Kicking himself in the ass wasn't helping. His hands were tied. The only thing he could do was pray she contacted him and let him know she was okay. He couldn't put an APB out on her because she wasn't in WITSEC. He couldn't report her as a missing person because he risked alerting a crooked cop with the wrong contacts. He also couldn't use any of his snitches and connections he'd been cultivating for the past six months—he didn't know any of them well enough to trust them with Harper's life—so he was out of options.

When his phone rang, he jabbed the Bluetooth connect button on his steering wheel without looking at the radio to see what number the call was from. His hope that it was Harper plummeted when Carson's voice came through the speakers. "Quinn? You there?"

He sighed heavily. "Yeah, I'm here. What's up?"

There was a slight pause. "What's wrong? You sound like you're having a bad day."

"That's an understatement, but it's nothing I can

discuss over the phone, and nothing you have to worry about. What's up?" he repeated.

"I just wanted to let you know plans have changed. We've gotten a bunch of patients from the riots and a five-car pileup on the interstate. I have no idea what time I'll be getting out of here. They've just started diverting all non-critical patients to other hospitals until further notice." It wasn't an uncommon occurrence, happening about once a month when San Francisco General got overloaded. "I'll call you when I have a better idea of what time I'll be home. Maybe we'll just do pizza tonight, okay?"

"Yeah, that's fine. The way my day is turning out, staying in sounds great."

"Anything I can—hang on. What?" That last word was fainter, and Quinn realized Carson was holding the phone away from his mouth, talking to someone else. A moment later he was back. "I'm sorry, Quinn. I've got to run. I'll call you later when I get a chance. Stay safe."

"I will. Love you, babe."

"Love you too. Gotta go."

"Bye."

Unsure of what to do at that point, Quinn headed back to the office. If he couldn't find Harper, he'd have to try and work it from the other end. To start, he'd try to find out how much Frankie-boy had upped the offer to send his sister to an early grave.

AFTER PUTTING TWO LEFTOVER SLICES OF WHITE, vegetable pizza in the refrigerator, Carson glanced around the kitchen and made sure there was nothing else that needed to be done before wandering back into the living room. Quinn was sitting on their L-shaped couch with one leg stretched out on the cushions and the other bent, with his foot on the floor. Carson laid down between them and placed his head on Quinn's thigh, tucking his hand underneath it. The TV was tuned to ESPN where the Giants were beating the Diamondbacks down in Arizona by six runs, but neither man was really paying attention to the game.

Quinn subconsciously stroked Carson's shoulder and upper arm. The marshal had been quiet throughout dinner, and, although he wanted to know what was going on, Carson had given him time to work through whatever was going on in his head. So, instead of asking questions, he'd talked about his day at the hospital. But now that dinner was over and they'd settled down, he'd try to get Quinn to open up. Carson probably wouldn't be of much help if it was work related, but sometimes just talking about it out loud helped. "So, what happened at work that had you out of sorts earlier?"

Taking a deep breath, Quinn let it out slowly. "Remember that woman I helped a while back? The one who opted out of the program, and I showed her how to stay under the radar."

While Carson hadn't known any of the details,

he'd gotten the basics. "Yeah. What happened? She okay?"

"She's been living in the city and ended up on TV after walking by a reporter and camera crew covering the riots." Carson winced as Quinn continued. "I just happened to see it at work. I went and got her at her job and had to leave her at her place, packing, to go cover another fucking bomb threat at the courthouse."

"I heard there was a live device this time."

"Yup. The disposal unit took care of it. But by the time I got back to the witness, someone had kicked in her door, and she was gone."

Carson sat up quickly and stared at Quinn. "Oh, shit! Was she—"

Quinn shook his head. "No. As far as I can tell, she made it out of there. Problem is I have no idea where she is. I was hoping she'd call. I can't put an APB or missing person report out on her. I've got a contact monitoring the police dispatch. He'll let me know if any homicides are called in. But, honestly, I think she's in the wind."

"Would anyone at her job know where she might have gone?"

"I doubt anyone would . . . "

Narrowing his eyes at the trailed off words, Carson asked, "What is it?"

Seconds ticked by, but it was clear Quinn was working things out in his head. Finally, he nodded. "There might be someone who can help. I'll have to check him out in the morning. He's not a guarantee, but you never know."

The look in Quinn's eyes said he was hopeful that whoever he'd just thought of could help solve the mystery of where the woman had gone, and he seemed to relax a little. Maybe Carson could ease some more of the tension from his Dom's body. Shifting onto his belly, Carson ran his hands up Quinn's muscular thighs, stopping at the creases of his pelvis and causing the man to growl. "What are you doing?"

"If it pleases you, Sir, I'd like to blow your mind, so to speak."

Quinn smirked as his cock twitched in his loose sweatpants. His nostrils flared at the same time lust bloomed in his eyes. "Is that so?"

"Yes, Sir," the sub responded with a seductive yet playful grin. "I think my Master could use some relaxation right about now."

It only took a moment before Quinn gave a single nod of his head. "Do your best."

"Always."

Pulling on the drawstring at Quinn's waist, Carson loosened it, then shimmied the material down until the glorious cock that belong to him appeared. It was a thing of beauty and made his mouth water. Wrapping his hand around the thick stalk, he opened his lips and leaned forward. Quinn gasped then moaned as his cock disappeared into his lover's mouth. He thrust his hand into Carson's hair and tightened, lighting up the nerves in his scalp and making him as hard as his Dom was. He ignored it, though, tonight was about taking care of his Master instead of the reverse. While Carson would always be the submissive in their relationship, he did enjoy when the control was handed over to him, albeit for a brief moment in time.

Sucking the tip to the back of his throat, Carson swallowed.

Quinn's hips bucked. "Fuck! Do it again! Damn, I love when you do that."

After swallowing two more times, Carson curled his tongue around Quinn's dick, laving the thick vein on the underside in earnest. His grip eased and tightened around the root of the hard flesh while his other hand cupped Quinn's balls, rolling them gently. Salty pre-cum teased Carson's taste buds. He'd never get tired of giving his Dom blowjobs. The only thing he loved more was having Quinn's cock buried deep in his ass.

Bobbing his head up and down, Carson glanced up at Quinn's face. Through narrow slits, the man's gaze was glued to where they were joined. He fucked Carson's mouth, moaning his pleasure. "Faster, baby. Damn that feels so good."

Still cupping Quinn's balls, Carson straightened his middle finger and rubbed the sensitive tissue behind them, near the man's anus. His eyes slamming shut, Quinn squirmed at the new sensation, and the grip he had on Carson's hair tightened further, urging him to go faster and deeper.

Quinn panted for air, and his body went rigid a split second before the first streams of cum shot to the back of Carson's throat. He eagerly swallowed every drop, then licked Quinn clean as the man's body went lax. Heaving for oxygen, Quinn let go of his sub's hair. "Come here, babe."

Crawling, Carson moved forward as Quinn sat up and pulled him close. Their mouths met, and Quinn's tongue immediately forged an invasion. He devoured Carson who quickly figured out the evening was far from over. Thank God because, now, he was the one dying for release.

CHAPTER EIGHT

"... Has told CBS News that details of the kidnapping of San Francisco Police Chief Tom Brown's adult daughter are not being released at this time. Nicole Brown has been missing since, at least, last night, but her last known location is still being investigated. Stay tuned to CBS News for more—"

Quinn shut off his pickup's engine, silencing the radio. He had his own missing person case to deal with. Jumping out of his pickup truck, he slammed the driver's door and jogged across the parking lot. It hadn't taken long to find out what precinct Detective Aidan "Mac" MacKenzie worked at, after Quinn had gone back to Del Mar to find out his name. Thankfully, her coworkers were a chatty bunch.

While it wasn't the first time Harper had used Quinn as her "boyfriend," this time hadn't been to dissuade some random asshole from hitting on her.

Whether she was willing to admit it or not, Mac meant something to her. Quinn just hoped the feelings were mutual, because he'd run out of options. Harper was nowhere to be found.

Running a frustrated hand through his hair, he slowed his stride as he approached the double doors to the building, which slid open as he stepped on the large trigger mat in front of them. Before he'd left the condo this morning, he'd made a few discreet calls and found out Frankie had upped the bounty on his sister's head. Every greedy hitman with contacts in the Russo organization would be out looking for her.

The lobby was empty, but there was a harried-looking, uniformed officer sitting at a desk behind a pane of bullet-proof glass. He was on the phone and his voice was muffled as he tried to get whomever was on the other end to listen to him. He raised an eyebrow at Quinn, who pulled his sports coat back just far enough to flash his shield, but not enough for the other man to get a good look at it. "I'm here to see Detective MacKenzie."

As expected, the cop nodded, as he tried to get a word in with whomever was annoying the crap out of him, and hit a hidden button under the desk. A buzzing sounded as the wooden door to Quinn's left unlocked. Waving his thanks, he grabbed the doorknob with his other hand and pulled it open. There was a long hallway with multiple open and closed doors on either side. Another uniformed cop, this one older and gray-haired, came out from one with a stack of files. Quinn flagged him down. "Hey, I'm supposed to meet Detective MacKenzie, but it's my first time here. Do you know where I can find him?"

"Yeah, I think he's at his desk. End of the hall, take a left, first door on your right."

"Thanks."

Quinn walked into the Detective Bureau and the receptionist pointed to a cubicle when he asked if MacKenzie was in. He strode across the room just as the man he was looking for stood from his desk with a cup of coffee in his hand. When he spotted Quinn, his expression turned hard, anger and jealousy flaring in his eyes. The marshal ignored the attitude—he didn't have time for it. "You got a minute?"

MacKenzie's brow furrowed. "Nope. I'm on a case. And don't bother coming back, because I don't have a goddamn thing to say to you."

When the detective attempted to walk around him, Quinn brought a hand up and stopped him in his tracks. "She's gone."

"Who the fuck are you talkin' about?" he asked, looking like he wanted to break Quinn's hand and rip his head off his shoulders, in that order.

"Laura. She took off."

Scoffing, the man knocked the hand away from his chest. "And? Man, that's not my business. Don't bother me with your domestic issues."

Once more, he tried to circumvent Quinn, but this time the marshal stepped in front of him, glancing around to see who was nearby. While the other detectives appeared to be busy, there was no doubt they had one ear listening to the conversation taking place in the middle of their bullpen. "Is there someplace we can talk in private?"

"I have someplace I have to be," he spat. "Now get the hell out of my way."

Quinn stared at the man, but didn't move. "She didn't tell you, did she?"

"Who are you?" A thought seemed to pop into the detective's mind. "And how the hell did you get back here without an escort?"

He lowered his voice. "Deputy Quinn Alexander, US Marshal."

MacKenzie's eyes narrowed again. "Come again?"

"Can you dial down your jealousy a few notches for five damn minutes? We need to talk in private," Quinn demanded with a glare. "Now." If he didn't need this asshole's help so badly, he would've stormed out of there or decked the guy—it was still up for grabs which action would have won the battle raging within him.

The same battle seemed to be warring in the other man's head, too. Seconds ticked by before he finally nodded. "This way."

Quinn followed him into an interrogation room and shut the door behind them. They stood across from one another, a scratched and dented metal table between them, but neither sat down on any of the three mismatched chairs.

"What can I do for you, *Deputy?*" MacKenzie crossed his arms over his chest, but didn't hide the fact his hands were clenched in fists.

"When was the last time you saw Laura?"

"At the café. Right before she left with you."

Quinn fought the urge to tell him to knock off the jealous attitude again. He studied the detective for a moment. It was obvious there were a few things, if not more, the man was unaware of when it came to the woman he'd been sleeping with. Harper may have been with Mac for the better part of a year, but she still hadn't told him who she really was. "What did she tell you about her past?"

Confusion replaced the other emotions. "I'm not real fond of being interrogated, so why don't you cut to the chase? If you're asking me if I know where your woman is—I don't. She never was good at answering her phone when I called. Guess I now know why."

"She loves you," Quinn blurted, putting up his hand to stop MacKenzie from protesting. "She lied to you the other day. I'm not her boyfriend—not by a long shot." Quinn snorted. "She's not my type, so to speak. I was in charge of getting her settled in WITSEC."

"What? WITSEC?"

"Witness Security—"

"I know what the fucking program is," he interrupted with an eye roll, before focusing his glare on Quinn once more. "Why would Laura be in WITSEC?"

Quinn didn't answer right away. If Harper had been in the program, what he was about to do would have gotten him in deep shit—hell, even fired—but she'd forced his hand and, once again, he was out of options. *Shit, I hope I'm doing the right thing, because if I'm wrong, she's a dead woman.*

His gaze flitted to the stained ceiling tiles above the table, and he let out an exasperated breath. "I'm only telling you this because I know she loves you, even if she won't admit it. And, by the look of devastation on your face when she lied and said she was involved with me, I'd say you love her too." When MacKenzie opened his mouth, Quinn held up a hand. "Don't bother denying it, because I really don't want to hear it. What I need is for you to shut up and listen." Not giving the man a chance to react, Quinn said, "Her real name is Harper Russo. Ring any bells?"

He waited a few seconds, and when there wasn't a response, he continued. "Her brother is Frankie Russo—of the Long Island, New York, Russos." Quinn saw the moment MacKenzie recognized the name—his eyes grew a little wider, and his mouth fell open a fraction of an inch. "He took over for his father after the old man was whacked at the family's pizzeria. Marco Russo was as close to a good-guy boss as you can find in the mob. Frankie? Exact opposite. All the things his father kept off the table—a stable of girls, human trafficking, high interest loans—Frankie not only put them back on the table but demanded his soldiers deliver."

Quinn stopped for a moment and sat in the metal chair stretching his legs out in front of him. *Might as well get comfortable. This will take a few minutes.*

"Harper saw something she wasn't supposed to. Frankie was pissed, to put it mildly. They argued, but she wouldn't change her point of view on the situation, so Frankie did what he does best; he tried to physically convince her to see things his way."

MacKenzie shook his head as if he were trying to prevent his disbelief from becoming a certainty. "The scars on her legs."

"Yeah—nice fucking brother, huh? She held out as long as she could. Frankie left her on the floor of one of his warehouses. He thought he'd killed her and called in a soldier to dump her body somewhere and make it look like a rival did it. In an unusual act of humanity, the soldier dropped her off behind a police station and called 9-1-1 to report where he'd left her. From what I heard, when Frankie found out she was still alive and with the feds, he made an example of the soldier. As you can imagine, it wasn't pretty."

Quinn gave the other man a few moments to digest everything, and knew what he had to be thinking. Who the fuck did that to their own family?

When MacKenzie's shock morphed into anger, he growled, "Where the fuck is she?"

"Good, it's finally sinking in—it's about fucking

time. That's why I am here, Detective. Harper . . . Laura . . . was inadvertently caught on a news broadcast reporting the riots around the city. She was in the background crossing the street, but she was on camera long enough for me to immediately recognize her. And if I recognized her, that means there's a possibility one of Frankie's guys did too. They have a million reasons to be on the lookout for her. Frankie went all out this time—a cool mil to kill his sister. Or he himself could've seen her on TV. Who knows? It's not like he has much else to do sitting on his ass in the penn. However small the chance, it was still too big—I couldn't risk her life assuming no one else saw her. I needed to warn her, and she needed to leave the city immediately. That's why I went to Del Mar's. It was sheer coincidence I'd transferred to the area from San Diego a few months ago—not that I can't say I'm not thankful for the good luck."

MacKenzie's eyes bore into Quinn and suspicion filled his voice. "How'd you know where she was if she'd refused WITSEC?"

"Just because she refused, didn't mean I was going to throw her to the wolves. I trained her how to stay off the grid and how to disappear, if needed. Unfortunately, I may have taught her too well because I can't find her." Quinn paused, hating to say his next words but the guy was in love with Harper and had a right to know. "I had an emergency call and had to leave her to pack up her stuff. I gave her the address to a safehouse if she had to split. When I got back to her place about three hours later, the door had been kicked in. From the evidence at the scene, she got away, but someone knew where to find her in the first place. And she's not at the safehouse, nor is she answering her phone. I had a contact try to track it, but it's turned off. With her not in the program, my hands are tied. If I fill out a missing person report on her, that opens a whole new can of worms that can't be closed again."

Pulling a business card out of the inside breast pocket of his sports coat, Quinn placed it on the table. "I read your file earlier before making the decision to come here. Accommodations, medals, fast tracked to detective—all and all, you look like a damn good cop. I hope that's not just on paper. I can't use my office or federal resources to track Harper. Officially your hands are as tied as mine, but I'm sure you have connections in the city I don't—not up here, not yet. If we're going to find Harper before they do, I'll need you to call in some markers."

The detective snarled, clearly still pissed at Harper or the situation and taking it out on the only person he could at the moment. "There's no we, in this. I don't know you."

Quinn was about to protest, but MacKenzie ignored him and strode toward the door. He stopped with his hand on the doorknob and pulled it before glancing back over his shoulder. "You said you just transferred up here, yeah?" Quinn nodded, unsure where this was going. "Don't you have boxes to unpack or paper clips to link together?"

His jaw clenched as he stood from the chair, trying to keep his own anger in check. There was always a rivalry between local cops and the feds, but this time it was personal. He closed the distance between them. "I'm feeling rather generous this morning. I'll give you a pass on your bullshit, this once. I get that she hurt you, and she used me to do it. Get the fuck over yourself, and hurry. Harper's out there alone with a bounty on her pretty, little head. Call me when you've figured out you need me more than you think you do."

Shouldering his way past the other man, Quinn hoped like hell MacKenzie got his head out of his ass and found the woman he loved before it was too late.

CHAPTER NINE

D_amn it!_ Quinn was ready to send his cell phone flying out the passenger window, but he needed it. He'd felt it vibrate on his hip but had been unable to answer it as he'd been escorting a high-profile witness from the federal courthouse with Owens, Brighton, and Szymanski. It wasn't until they were on the highway and it appeared no one was following them on their way to a safehouse, that Quinn had been able to check his phone. There'd been no voice message left, but he'd been able to trace the phone number to a payphone near Lake Tahoe—it had to have been Harper. He didn't know anyone, personally or professionally, in that area. He was just about to call Detective MacKenzie when the phone vibrated in his hand. Glancing at the screen, he saw it was a local but unfamiliar number.

"Deputy Alexander."

"It's Mac," came the response.

Well, speak of the devil. "You get one too?" If the man had also received a call, he'd understand the stilted question.

"I did." There was a slight pause and then, "I need to apologize. I was a dick, and you were right; my head was up my own ass."

"No need." He checked the passenger sideview mirror for any signs they'd picked up a tail, as Owens drove, following Brighton and Szymanski who had the witness in their vehicle. "Missed my call. I'm wrapped up in something that's unavoidable." Mac didn't need to be a rocket scientist to figure that one out.

"I didn't miss mine. Maybe you should call me back when you get somewhere private. I'm good on my end."

In other words, Mac was on a secure phone while Quinn wasn't. There was no way to inquire if he'd actually spoken to Harper without worrying about an intercept, so instead, Quinn asked, "Are you driving?"

"About to. I have a few days off—thought I'd get some fresh air." Mac must have been with someone because Quinn heard him talking away from the phone but couldn't make out what was said until he spoke into the mouthpiece again. "Seems I have company. I'd better go. Call when you can."

Without giving Quinn a chance to respond, the detective hung up. His voice had sounded cautious but not too worried, so Quinn hoped that meant Mac could get to Tahoe, and Harper, without being followed. From everything Quinn had heard, Mac knew his shit—he better, for Harper's sake.

Five hours later, using one of his burner phones, Quinn dialed the number Mac had called him from earlier. Quinn didn't have much time; he and Owens would be busy for the rest of the night—the FBI had a new witness for them—but he needed to know if Mac had found Harper.

The phone rang twice before it was connected, and the baritone voice he'd been expecting came over the line. "Mac."

"You got the package?"

"Yes." Short and to the point.

Quinn sighed in relief. "Good. I'm going to be out of reach for a while—work related. I trust you have the situation under control."

"I do."

The door to the office opened, and four federal agents and one nervous-looking squirrel of a man walked in. Quinn turned his back on them for a moment. "I'll be in touch when I can. Tell her I hope she understands why I told you."

Without waiting for an answer, Quinn hung up. It was highly unlikely their communication had been intercepted, but he didn't want to risk giving someone a chance to triangulate the call and locate Mac and Harper. Popping the back of the phone off, he yanked out the battery and SIM card, breaking the latter in half before tossing everything into his desk drawer and locking it until he could dispose of it later. Then, before he joined Owens and the newcomers in the office conference room, he popped one of the pills he'd been prescribed by the doctor Carson had insisted he see. Apparently, Quinn had a small ulcer that had been causing his heartburn. The pills helped, but he'd also had to make some changes to his diet. Not that he'd been eating unhealthy choices often, but some of the spicier foods he enjoyed were out for now. The third thing the gastroenterologist had encouraged was to reduce the stress Quinn's job had placed on him. Until he found something in the private sector, though, he was stuck here. He just hoped the stress didn't kill him before a good job offer came his way.

"HEY, NICK, THANKS FOR CALLING ME BACK." Carson lowered the volume on the TV as he held his cell phone to his ear with his other hand. Quinn had called about ten minutes ago and had said he'd be home in an hour. Instead of ordering takeout again, Carson had cooked chicken and fresh vegetables. He'd already eaten but was keeping the food warm for Quinn.

"No problem, dude, what's up? How're the waves?"

Carson chuckled. "Good. Managed to catch some good ones this morning. How are things in Tampa?"

"I wouldn't know. I'm on an assignment, but I've got a few minutes to chat."

Since Nick hadn't said where he was, Carson assumed he was doing the same thing he'd done while in the SEALs and didn't press. "If you're sure . . ."

"Yeah, no problem. What's up?" the other man repeated.

"Um . . . I've got a favor to ask, but I'm not sure how it'll be received. I'm not sure how this all works in the military, law enforcement, or private security worlds, so if I'm making a faux pas, just tell me. Quinn doesn't know I'm talking to you. He's been looking into leaving the Marshals . . . the stress is getting to him. He can't change his need to do something along those lines, so he's been putting out feelers in the private sector, but there doesn't seem to be much in the area. We talked about it, and he doesn't want me to give up my position, so anything he took would have to be here. I was wondering if you or your brothers knew of anyone hiring . . . you know, through channels."

"Shit. Hang on a sec . . ."

There was a brief flash of worry that Carson had stepped on Nick's toes by asking, but then he heard the man talking to someone else in the background of the call. After a few moments he came back on the line. "Sorry about that. Um . . . personally, I don't have those contacts, at least not yet, but Ian and Dev do. Too bad San Diego's out, 'cause he could've come onboard with TS West. I can ask my brothers if they can get him a leg in somewhere but I won't be in contact with them for a few more days."

"No rush. Quinn will need a good six to eight weeks to hand over his cases before he can leave anyway. I appreciate any help your brothers could give him.

"I made appointments at the hospital for his heartburn and a stress test. The cardiology reports were good, but he does have a small ulcer the gastroenterologist is now treating with prescription acid reducers and a better diet."

"So, he needs something that will challenge him but not kill him—gotcha. I'll see what I can find out and get back to you when I can."

"Thanks. Oh, and we loved the wedding photos. Looked like you all had a great time. Sorry we had to miss it."

"Shit happens. Whoops, gotta go. I'll talk to you soon."

The call disconnected before Carson could say goodbye, but it wasn't the first time Nick's job had required him to end a conversation abruptly. Now Carson had to decide whether to tell Quinn he'd called Nick or wait until he heard back from their friend. Either way, Carson was sure he had a punishment coming his way for not discussing it with his Dom in the first place. Good thing most of his punishments ended with an explosive orgasm.

CHAPTER TEN

Three weeks later...

AFTER SEEING HE'D MISSED A CALL WHILE IN THE shower, Quinn headed for the kitchen. He was sure he was going to need some coffee in him before he returned the it. He'd taken the morning off after working eight days straight between the usual caseload and the extra details that'd needed to be covered. The local marshals, FBI, and police had been busy thanks to all the riots and looting, the non-violent but large protests, and the bomber who'd finally been caught without any of his devices exploding. The guy had been pissed at his soon-to-be-ex-wife's father, who'd encouraged her to file for divorce and also happened to be a judge at the city's federal courthouse.

He'd been shocked last night when Jake Donovan had called and said his bosses, Nick's older brothers, wanted to know when they could meet with Quinn about a West Coast position with Trident Security. Apparently, Carson had spoken to Nick a few weeks ago to see if any of them had any connections in California's private sector. Carson hadn't expected them to offer him a job, just some help in pointing Quinn in the right direction. But wonders never ceased; while TS West was located in San Diego, there was a need for more operatives further up the coast. Not only was Quinn being considered for a job, but Devon and Ian Sawyer wanted to talk to him about running a San Francisco office with two or three employees to start off with. While Quinn was annoyed Carson hadn't said anything to him about his request to Nick, the Dom couldn't stay that way. His submissive had done it out of love and concern ford his health, and had the situation been reversed, Quinn probably would have done the same thing for him.

Having set up a formal interview for the following week, Quinn decided to still keep his intentions for leaving the Marshals quiet for now. He hadn't even told Owens yet, but his partner would be the first one to know if, and when, a resignation date was set—it was the right thing to do considering they'd worked side-by-side for months.

Once his coffee was ready, Quinn took the cup and sat at the dinette. Dialing the number for the missed call on a burner phone, he set his personal cell down and waited for the call to be answered, scanning the newspaper Carson had left for him on the table. As they had for weeks, the riots monopolized the front-page news. Fifteen more idiots had been arrested yesterday for assault, vandalism, and/or theft, while numerous injuries had been reported.

"Quinn. Thanks for calling me back," Mac said by way of a greeting when he answered the call. "You're on speaker. Reid's here."

Logan Reid was a private investigator who'd gone with Mac to find Harper near Tahoe. They'd gotten there just in time since one of the hitmen looking for her had been about to kill her. He ended up dead, and Harper had managed to survive with just some bumps and bruises. Several days later, Quinn had gotten word that Frankie Russo had been shanked in prison. The deputy didn't believe in coincidences, but sometimes it was better not knowing the details. He suspected Mac had, somehow, had a hand in the mobster's death, but there was no way Quinn was going to ask. In fact, had he been in Mac's shoes, Quinn may have very well done the same thing— whatever it'd been. If Carson had a million-dollar price on his head, Quinn would have done anything to ensure his safety—even make a deal with the devil.

Since Harper was safely back in his arms, Mac had thanked Quinn for his help, then surprised the marshal by asking for a favor in return. The detective had been assigned a case his chief had demanded no details be released to the public. But things didn't add up, and Mac had filled Quinn in, suspecting he'd need help outside the SFPD at some point. Sooner or later, the shit was going to hit the fan.

"It sounded important," Quinn replied, pushing the newspaper to the side.

"Are we secure?"

"From my end, yes."

"I have confirmation Graham Cartwright is trying to renegotiate payoffs." That was political bomb number one. Graham Cartwright was San Francisco's District Attorney. He was in deep with the underbelly of San Francisco—drug dealers, a motorcycle gang, and even the local mob—greed made strange bedfellows. Cartwright wanted the payoffs others were getting after finding out his take was less than theirs. And that led to the second bomb. Apparently several other high-profile figures and local police officers could also be connected to the criminal population of San Francisco—one of them being Tom Brown, chief of the city's police department. Both men had their hands dirty, but not necessarily together. In the chief's case, he'd racked up a shit-ton of gambling debts. His daughter had been kidnapped and was being held until he paid the money he owed to the local mob—not that those facts had been released by the police department. Brown couldn't let that fact go public, so he'd called Mac in to work the case, but had left out numerous details, which the detective had slowly been uncovering. What worried Quinn was how the chief was going to ensure his subordinate's silence if the young woman was rescued —something Mac was wondering about as well.

"The DA's hit up a few of the powerhouses in the drug trade and has started moving down the ladder, approaching the up and comers. I'm concerned about the mid-level players. They don't have a mind for proper etiquette yet and are reckless. They believe they can catapult themselves into the big game by a show of force. That often times leads to innocent people getting caught in the melee."

Reid took over from there. "I have taps on both of their home phones and cells. Seems the DA isn't trying to hide what he's doing, moving into the chief's business. Either he doesn't care or knows that Brown is going down and won't be able to stop him from taking his payoffs. At first, I thought he just wanted a bigger cut of the action but that's not it. He's making moves to take over completely. I highly doubt that Brown's had a sudden change of heart and decided to go on the straight and narrow."

"You think the DA is planning on taking Brown out?" Quinn asked.

"That's one assumption. But I haven't heard anything on the wire about a hit being put out. That'd be a big contract and Dustin's been monitoring all assets. There's been no chatter." Dustin was Reid's computer analyst and hacker.

Quinn thought about that for a moment. The

main reason Mac had pulled him into this mess was because he needed a federal contact he could trust when the time came for warrants and arrests. The police chief thought Mac had been quietly investigating the missing woman, but what he didn't know was the detective was also building a case to ferret out the corruption going on at all levels of the San Francisco criminal justice arena.

Grabbing a pen Carson had been using to do the newspaper's crossword while eating his breakfast, Quinn twirled it through his fingers. "What about the girl? Any closer to finding her yet?"

There was a longer pause than he expected before Mac responded, "I am. I have a pretty good idea where she is."

It took Quinn a moment to realize the man wasn't going to elaborate. "Are you gonna share?"

Again, a longer pause than necessary. "Not yet. Give me a few more days."

His eyes narrowed, and he couldn't keep the annoyed tone from his voice. "What is it you need from me then?"

"I can't trust my department. I don't know who Brown has on his sideline payroll—and I'm sure he has some because he'd need people on the inside to cover his tracks. I need warrants. Everything I have so far would be considered fruit of the poisonous tree. The taps we have in place aren't exactly legal—nothing we've gained from them will be admissible."

"And what exactly do you have?" If Quinn was

going to be sticking his finger in an electrical socket, he wanted to know how badly he might get burned first.

Reid was the one to lay out the details. "Brown's been talking about the 500K he's into Tuscani for." Nico Tuscani was the head of the mob that dominated the San Francisco underworld. "He's also trying to work out a deal with a gangbanger Evan Johnson. White boy from Sacramento who goes by the street name of 'Loco.' Grew up in the Fivers' territory and worked his way up. One of the few white kids that's made it into a position of power in a Mexican gang. His mother being half-Guatemalan was his in."

"Fivers? Word is it was a Fiver that killed Holly Springs." And sparked the city-wide unrest.

"That's correct. They're trying to branch out into Oakland and San Francisco. They're also responsible for some of the riots. They've been showing up at the vigils for Holly and the protests demanding the police do more to stop the gangs. The Fivers stir up trouble, and the peaceful protests turn violent.

"I checked Brown's background," the private detective continued. "He has control of an account in his ex-wife's maiden name, and in the last month there have been large deposits from a bank in Sacramento. After the last conversation Brown had with Johnson, there was a deposit for $50K from the same bank. That was the exact amount they'd agreed on."

"So, what's Brown's end of the deal?" Quinn asked as he heard the sound of papers being rustled on the other end of the line.

"He's allowing the Fivers to move in on Tuscani's territory."

The marshal let out a low whistle. "That's not going to end well. Tuscani will burn the city down." Double crossing Nico was not a wise thing to do. Tom Brown would end up in a shallow grave next to his daughter faster than you could roast a pig on a spit—pun intended.

"Fuck me," Mac muttered before raising his voice again. "How fast do you think you can get a few warrants?"

Quinn blew out a deep breath. "Not long. Do you need one for Cartwright too?"

"No. I have his balls nailed to the wall. I'm holding off taking him until we have everything set with Brown. I don't want to tip our hand and spook the DA. We need to take them both at the same time."

"You never did tell me what evidence you had on Cartwright," Reid said to Mac.

"Cartwright bribed Judge Barnes to railroad Jason Riggers. It was an easy trail to follow. Let's just say Barnes owed me a favor. All it took was a little nudge, and he sang like a canary. He knew he was fucked and didn't want to spend his golden years in the penn. He's a smart old man and kept emails and voicemails he'd received from the DA, and he's got dirt on fifteen other judges, past and present, who are in Cartwright's pocket. Barnes is ready to strike a deal."

Quinn realized he was going to need some help with this. "I'm going to have to bring my partner, Bryan Owens, in on this—he's got the intel and contacts I don't have yet. He's going to want to know which judges are out, so he knows who's safe to approach. It might take a couple of days. I want to be certain whomever we go to isn't going to throw us to the wolves. What are you going to do with Barnes? Do I need to pick him up and put him somewhere until we can sort through the charges and round everyone up?"

"That's a good idea," the detective concurred. "This is a need-to-know operation—only people you trust. We have to assume Brown and Cartwright have eyes and ears everywhere."

"Agreed."

"Be safe. Call if you need me."

"Later." Quinn disconnected the call, then, still using the burner phone, he dialed another number.

The call was answered after the third ring. "Owens."

"Hey, it's Quinn. We need to talk."

CHAPTER ELEVEN

Quinn paced on the sidewalk in front of Judge Fox's house. He was a justice on the state supreme court, and lived in the upper-class neighborhood of Presidio Heights. Quinn stilled as a black pickup pulled up to the curb, and the engine was shut off. Mac climbed out of the truck and approached him, carrying a file box. Since he was alone, Quinn figured Reid would be along shortly as Mac had said they'd both meet him here.

"Thanks for coming on such short notice," Quinn greeted him.

"I'm the one who should be thanking you. Before we go in, what can you tell me about Fox?" Mac eyed what was, more than likely, a twenty-million-dollar home that belonged to the judge.

Quinn could almost hear the gears spinning in the cop's head. "I know what you're thinking. Judge Fox comes from money, as did his late wife. Owens says

Fox can be trusted, but I still looked into him. Called a black-ops friend in Tampa who works with one of the best hackers around. The guy could probably tell you every digital footprint Fox has ever left, plus what time he takes a shit every day. Everything Owens told me checked out—the judge is clean."

Not wanting to raise any flags here in San Francisco, Quinn had contacted Jake, who'd gotten the okay from Ian Sawyer to help the marshal out. Even though they were in the private sector, Trident still had black-ops contracts with the US government. Quinn knew when he asked them to keep the investigation buried, it wouldn't go any further than the Trident headquarters. In fact, Jake had offered to have some of the operatives from TS West head up to the city from San Diego if they were needed, but Quinn didn't want to pull in any more people than necessary.

Another vehicle, this one a Land Rover, pulled up and parked behind the pickup. A man, presumably Mac's private detective friend, climbed out of the driver's seat, shut the door, and walked over to join them. Mac made the introductions. "Quinn Alexander, this is Logan Reid."

"Pleasure," Reid said and offered his hand, which Quinn shook.

"Nice to meet you." The marshal wasn't about to tell either man he'd had Jake's teammate investigate Reid too. If Quinn was putting his ass on the line, he wanted to make sure he knew who he could trust.

"What can you tell us about Fox?" It didn't go unnoticed that Reid was sizing up the mansion just as his buddy had.

Chuckling, Quinn glanced at Mac, then back to the other man. "Damn, you two think alike. I was explaining to Mac before you got here—Fox checked out. The money's from family. I had a black-ops friend, whom I trust implicitly, discreetly dig through the judge's financials. He's squeaky clean. As far as we can tell, he doesn't even take all the tax deductions he should. Either his accountant sucks or he doesn't mind paying the extra money to the government. Owens—my partner—his mother was good friends with the judge's mother, and both were members of the American Legion Ladies Auxiliary." Reid raised an eyebrow at that. It wasn't often you found a well-to-do woman at the beer and wings nights at the local legion. "Mrs. Fox passed away a few years ago, but the families are still in touch."

"How are we gonna play this?" Reid asked, but before either of the two men could answer him another vehicle pulled up. Both Quinn and Reid turned to scrutinize the driver.

Reid pulled his sunglasses off to get a better look. "Is that Larry Barnes?"

"Sure is," Mac responded.

"Your ace?"

"Yep."

"Care to fill me in?" Quinn glared at Mac, not

pleased with the surprise of another player he hadn't been aware of.

"Judge Barnes is here to guarantee our warrants." Mac pivoted toward the new man joining them without further explanation. "Larry."

"Afternoon, Detective." It was obvious Barnes was less than thrilled to be there. It also hadn't escaped Quinn's notice that Mac had called the judge by his first name and not "your Honor" as most were referred to in professional company.

Quinn wanted to know what the hell this judge was doing here when they already had Judge Fox, who was willing to sign the warrants once the evidence was laid out for him. But the little group was starting to draw attention from two women walking along the other side of the street with a baby in a stroller. Quinn gestured toward the long drive leading up to the house. "Why don't we take this inside. Owens is with the judge."

Moments later, without bothering to knock, Quinn let himself in through the unlocked front door. The others followed him in silence down a corridor that led to the back of the house. The inside of the massive home was even more majestic than the exterior. Mahogany wainscoting paneling gave a rich warm feel to the hall which opened into a library that was equally impressive. The gray-haired Judge Fox was seated behind an ornate desk, while Quinn's partner sat on a nearby brown, leather sofa. Both men stood and didn't hide their surprise when Judge Barnes walked in with the others.

Once the introductions were made all around, everyone took seats on either the couch or one of the several chairs in the room. Fox took his original position behind his desk and didn't bother with any chit-chat. "Deputies Alexander and Owens gave me a preliminary outline. However, before I can issue an arrest warrant for the District Attorney of San Francisco, I need more than assumption and conjecture." With a frown, he regarded Mac. "You do understand the implications of your accusations if you're wrong? It won't just be you, Detective, on the receiving end of a reprimand. I, too, will be held accountable. While my interest is certainly piqued, and I've heard rumors over the years, I will not risk my career or Graham Cartwright's based on rumor. Please tell me you have solid evidence to back up your accusations."

"I do your Honor. Judge Barnes?" Mac motioned for the man to tell everyone where he fit into all of this.

Barnes looked pale and tired. The resignation in his voice was evident, even to Quinn who'd just met him. "You have to know I'm deeply ashamed of my actions," Barnes began. "Ten years ago, I paid for sexual favors from a woman who was provided by an escort service. Shortly thereafter, I was approached by Graham Cartwright." The man paused for a moment, a pained expression crossing his face. Quinn almost felt sorry for him . . . almost. Barnes cleared his throat before continuing. "He had photographs of me in compromising positions with the prostitute. Cartwright began blackmailing me. In the beginning, it was small things like dismissing evidence a defense attorney presented. As the years went on, his demands increased." Barnes stopped and held his judicial colleague's angry stare.

"And what are his current demands?" Fox ground out.

Barnes's gaze dropped to the floor in defeat or embarrassment, or a combination of both. "His latest request was to charge Jason Riggers with aggravated assault and attempted murder."

"And?"

Licking his dry lips, Barnes swallowed hard. "Cartwright had no evidence to substantiate his allegations, but requested a bond hearing in my chambers, which I heard and denied the ROR and bond. Riggers is currently being held in California State Prison."

Holy shit! Quinn raised an eyebrow at Owens, who was shaking his head in disgust, as Fox asked, "Where was Mr. Riggers's attorney?"

"Cartwright failed to notify the defendant's counsel."

"So, the case will be thrown out. Right?"

There was no immediate answer, and Quinn was certain another bomb was coming, one that told how deep the corruption went into the system. Barnes shook his head. "Not if it's brought before me. Cartwright demanded I allow the case to be heard and do everything I can to make sure Riggers is found guilty of attempted murder. Then I'm supposed to give the maximum sentence allowed."

"Shit," Owens murmured. Mac, Reid, and Quinn remained silent, nodding their agreement. The maximum for attempted murder in the first degree was life in prison with the possibility of parole. But it was highly unlikely Riggers would ever step foot out of prison alive. Even if there was an appeal, the guy would probably be shanked before then.

Judge Fox's face was crimson, and Quinn was shocked he didn't actually see steam coming from the man's ears—he looked about to explode. "Jesus Christ, Larry." Fox ran a hand down his face in disbelief before pointing an angry finger at his colleague. "I want exact clarification; San Francisco's District Attorney, Graham Cartwright, told you outright, and in no uncertain terms, to fix the trial so the jury has no choice but to find Jason Riggers guilty of attempted murder in the first degree, even if the evidence didn't support the charge?"

Barnes sighed heavily. "Yes. And Riggers is only the latest."

Quinn hadn't thought it was possible for Fox's complexion to get any redder, but it did. His hands were clenched tightly where they rested on the desk. His voice was low, his anger barely controlled when he asked, "How many others?"

"Countless." He glanced at Mac, before addressing the other judge again. "I asked my clerk to bring ten boxes filled with case files to my home. Each box contains a year's worth of cases that Cartwright prosecuted in my courtroom. You'll have to subpoena the actual transcripts, but this will give you a head start. I'll save you the trouble of a search warrant and give you permission to enter and search my home. You'll find everything you need in my private office. I've already given Mr. Reid consent to wiretap my home, cell, and office phones and I've turned over voice recordings of conversations between Cartwright and myself, dating back to almost the beginning. Once I realized how bad it was going to get, I started recording everything. I knew it was only a matter of time. I know there's no excuse, but, at first, I was terrified my children would find out about the prostitute. It would have killed them after losing their mother. By the time I came to my senses, I was in too deep with Cartwright. I should have come clean a long time ago."

"But you stuck your fucking head in the sand and hoped it would just go away, but it didn't," Owens said distastefully.

Barnes bit his lip and nodded. "And I'm not the only one. I know of fourteen other judges, past and present, Cartwright has had in his pocket."

He pulled a folded piece of paper from the jacket of his sports coat and placed it on the desk. Wide-eyed, Fox picked it up and scanned a list of names. "Son of a bitch. There's proof?"

"I have enough to get you started on search warrants."

No one else spoke while Fox processed the information the now-disgraced judge had presented. Finally, Fox broke the silence, his fury barely leashed. "I want Cartwright behind bars within the hour. I will not stand for malversation. Anyone with any involvement with Cartwright's dirty practices will answer for their malfeasance.

"What do you want us to do about Chief Brown?" Reid asked Fox.

"Get Cartwright to flip on the chief, and I'll give you your warrant. I want every last charge to stick. Same goes for the names on this list—I want every T crossed and every I dotted. This is by the book. We cannot bend the law by the slightest fraction. I want ironclad arrests." Fox opened a manila folder that'd been sitting on his desk, pulled several forms out, and plucked a gold pen from its perch on a marble stand. After signing his name with a flourish to the pages that included search warrants for Cartwright's home and office, he tucked the papers back into the folder and handed it to Mac. "Does anyone know if this has to do with Brown's daughter's disappearance?"

Mac shrugged. "Is it possible? Hell yeah. Do we know for sure? No."

"Keep me posted and be safe, detective."

"Thank you, your Honor."

Quinn was surprised when Mac turned to Judge Barnes and held out his hand. "Thank you."

"Don't thank me—I don't deserve it."

The man was right, he didn't deserve the gratitude extended toward him. His testimony wasn't going to keep him out of prison, but it would probably reduce his sentence. His career had been over the minute he'd walked into the house. On top of that, he'd be sued by those "countless" people who'd been wrongfully convicted and sentenced to years of confinement. No, he definitely didn't deserve shit, but with his help, they'd be taking down the rest of them—like a line of dominoes.

CHAPTER TWELVE

"Dr. Patel, Dr. Matthews, there's an ambulance coming in with a GSW to the chest," an ER nurse called to the female emergency room physician and Carson. "No exit wound, unconscious, hypovolemic shock, airway secured." She hurried past them into the Trauma #1 to make sure it was ready. "It's a police detective."

"Shit," Carson muttered to himself. He'd been about to accompany the techs and nurses who were transporting a stab wound victim up to the OR after intubating him. He was starting to think he should have a second office in the ER since he'd been spending so much time there lately. Glancing at a respiratory tech who was using an ambu-bag to force air into the victim's lungs, he asked, "You okay taking him up? I'll stay for the GSW."

"No problem, Doc."

"Thanks. Just let them know I'll be down here if they need me."

"You got it."

Carson spun on his heel and walked back into the trauma room he'd just left moments before. After plucking two latex gloves from a nearby box, he pulled them on, then grabbed a new, sterile intubation kit from a cabinet and set it up on a clean tray near the head of an unoccupied gurney. Multiple sirens blaring announced the approach of the ambulance, and Carson followed two nurses, an orderly, and Dr. Patel out through the automatic bay doors just as the rig pulled in along with several police cars. The orderly swung open the ambulance's rear doors as the driver climbed out and rushed around to the back to help unload the stretcher.

As the patient was rolled inside and the EMTs were giving the patient's status to Dr. Patel, Carson spotted another man who'd jumped out the back of the rig. His hands were covered in blood, but it was evident it was from the patient and this man wasn't injured. Carson grabbed his arm before he jogged past to catch up with the stretcher. "Are you with him? Do you know him well?"

The man startled, and it took a moment for the questions to register. "Um, yeah. He's a friend."

Carson gestured toward the doors and started walking. "Great. I'm Dr. Matthews, the anesthesiologist. Is he allergic to anything?"

"No—not that I know of."

"Any medical conditions, taking any medications, vitamins?"

The man shook his head. "No conditions, no meds, and I don't know about the rest."

"All right. Thanks." Carson left him at the door to Trauma #1 and went to the head of the gurney as the patient was moved over from the stretcher on a backboard. As a female surgeon, Dr. Coats, strode into the room, Carson took care of the intubation.

Less than ten minutes later, the injured man was as stable as he was going to get as they rushed him up to the OR. In that short amount of time, the hospital had been inundated with both uniformed and plainclothes police officers. Carson had initially thought the shooting had been the result of a crime in progress or related to the ongoing riots, but he'd been as stunned as the staff when they'd heard the detective had been shot by Chief Tom Brown while trying to arrest the head of the police department. It was further learned that the chief and two other cops had been killed in the shootout. Carson was sure that was going to rock the already unstable city. Even though Quinn was federal, Carson was hoping the possible job with Trident Security worked out for him. Law enforcement in San Francisco had taken several hard hits over the past few weeks, and the press was going to have a field day with this new development. Things were going to get worse before they got better, and Carson prayed that no one he knew would get caught in the crossfire.

Quinn strode through the corridor filled with uniformed and plainclothes cops. He and Owens had been on a conference video for about two hours with deputies from the Dallas office and a witness who'd been relocated to San Francisco. The district attorney had wanted to go through the man's upcoming testimony in a few weeks. Once they'd finished, he'd checked his messages and found out Harper had called, crying. Quinn had cursed himself for not bringing his cell phone into the meeting, but it was what it was.

Upon entering the room, Quinn scanned the occupants and found Harper with Reid, another woman, and two children about six and eleven years old. As soon as he spotted Quinn approaching, Reid stood and held out his hand. "Hey, thanks for coming."

"No problem." Quinn shook the other man's hand, then hugged Harper when she got to her feet. "Are you okay?"

Her eyes were red from crying. "I'm hanging in there. It's just taking so long. He's been in there for over two hours."

"Mac's a strong man. He'll fight tooth and nail to come through this." He hugged her again and then let her return to her seat.

Turning to Reid, Quinn tilted his head toward the hallway and the other man followed. They moved to the far end of the corridor where they had a little bit of privacy. Keeping his voice low, Quinn asked, "What the hell happened?"

"Brown was waiting for us. Had two of his minions there too. Mac shot the two of them when they drew their weapons, then he took one to the chest from Brown's gun while pushing me out of the way. I killed the fucking bastard a second too late."

"Don't Monday morning quarterback. The what-if game sucks, and you'll never win. I know from experience. How bad's he hurt?"

Reid grimaced. "Bad. Coded in the ambulance but they managed to get him back."

"Shit." Quinn paused, trying to wrap his mind around the last twelve hours. "What about Cartwright? Is there enough to bring him down without Brown?"

"I don't know. I'm shut out of the investigation with Mac out of commission. And if it wasn't for body cam Mac had thought of putting on, I'd be knee deep in an interrogation right now."

Quinn's cell phone vibrated on his hip. He retrieved it and read the text from Owens. "Damn. This day just gets worse and worse. Gotta go move a witness. Can you call me and let me know how Mac's doing?"

"Yeah, sure."

Reaching over, he hit the down button for the elevator. "And if you or Harper need me for anything, don't hesitate."

Reid shook his hand again. "Thanks. I appreciate it."

As the other man walked back toward the OR waiting room, Quinn wondered if the job with Trident Security didn't work out, maybe he'd talk to Reid about working for him. But for now, he had too much going on to think about it. Sighing, he stepped onto the elevator and hit the lobby button. *Damn, I wish this day was just fucking over already.*

CARSON'S EYES ROLLED BACK INTO HIS HEAD AS Quinn entered him from behind. It was the second time this evening they'd made love, and it was just as intense as the first time before dinner. After polishing off the sushi Carson had picked up on the way home, they'd been lying naked on the couch, watching TV. Without a word, Quinn had suddenly flipped his sub onto his stomach, pulled his hips so Carson was on his knees, then reached for the tube of lubricant that had been left on the coffee table. If this was Quinn's new way of dealing with stress, instead of drawing into himself, Carson had no problem with it. He'd gladly give his Dom what he needed, if explosive orgasms were the end result— who wouldn't?

After coming out of the surgery for the police detective, Carson had been surprised to learn Quinn had been in the waiting room with the injured man's family, friends, and coworkers for a brief time before he'd gotten called away for a minor emergency at work. Over dinner, Quinn had filled him in on the abbreviated version of how he knew the detective. The rest of the story had been on the news. The city was stunned to learn the chief of police had been a crook who'd tried to kill the detective to keep his crimes hidden. While he'd only helped the detective from the sidelines, Quinn had, once again, felt guilty about how things had turned out. And, *once again*, Carson prayed things would work out for his lover moving into the private sector where it was, hopefully, safer and less stressful.

As Quinn thrust in and out of Carson's ass, his fingers dug into the sub's hips. Carson gasped and moaned as the drag of his lover's cock lit up the nerves of his rectum and stimulated his prostate. "God, that feels so freaking good. Don't stop."

Of course, Quinn did just that and slapped his Carson's ass cheek. "You don't give the orders, subbie. I'll stop and go as I please."

Swallowing hard, Carson fought the urge to rock his hips back to impale himself on the thick cock that was almost completely out of him at the moment. "Yes, Sir—it wasn't an order but a request."

One hand left Caron's hip and snaked around to wrap around his cock, while the fingernails of the other hand scraped down his bare back. Carson almost came right then and there. He didn't know what it was about getting his back scratched that turned him on something fierce, but it did. When Carson involuntarily clenched his ass in response to the combined erotic stimuli, Quinn plunged forward and resumed fucking him.

"That's my good subbie. So nice and fucking tight. Damn, I could fuck you forever and a day and still never tire of it."

"Thank God, because I know I'll never get enough either." It was the truth. There would never be another man who could capture and rule his heart, mind, and body like his Dom had. They'd talked about how they felt about marriage and kids a few times during their "getting to know you" period when they first started dating, but the subject hadn't come up in a while. Carson knew his friend Nick had been the one to propose to Jake, not knowing his Dom had been planning the same thing, but Carson wanted Quinn to be the one to propose. It was one of the things that made him a sub, needing to feel wanted. He needed to know Quinn wanted him to share his last name—*truly* wanted it—and not just because it was the next expected step in their relationship. He didn't want Quinn to ask because he felt cornered if Carson made it known he was waiting for a ring. Carson yearned for nothing more than to become Carson Matthews-Alexander, but if he had to wait for years until Quinn was ready than that's what he would do.

Minutes later, Quinn pulled out and flipped Carson onto his back, before spreading the man's legs wide and reentering him. The whole thing had been done in the blink of an eye, and once again Carson was in ecstasy.

"Jack off, babe," Quinn demanded as he thrust in and out like a piston from a NASCAR contender's engine.

Wrapping his hand tightly around his own cock, Carson did as ordered, and more pre-cum oozed from the tip. Quinn reached up and twisted one of his lover's taut nipples and that sent shockwaves through Carson. His hand pumped faster and harder as the need to cum grew to an unstoppable force. When Quinn tweaked his other nipple, it sent Carson over the edge. His eyes slammed shut as he shouted his release. Streams of cum landed on his taut abs and chest while fireworks went off in his mind. His orgasm caused Quinn to follow him into the abyss as the Dom slammed into him one last time and froze, emptying his seed deep in Carson's ass.

Gasping for air, Quinn collapsed on top of Carson, ignoring the mess between them. After taking a minute or two to recover, Quinn lifted his head, brushed his lips across Carson's, then held his sated stare with his own. "I love you, babe. Never doubt that for a moment. If something happened to either one of us, I don't ever want you to have questioned my love for you."

"I love you too—more than anything else in the world."

CHAPTER THIRTEEN

San Francisco—Oakland Bay Bridge 2 Miles. Quinn drove the federal-issued SUV past the sign announcing the span that would take them into the SF city limits and sighed in relief. He was beat, and so was Owens who'd just awoken from an hour-long snooze. The sun had set hours ago, and both men wanted nothing more than to get home and pass out in their own beds. The FBI had needed a witness moved after their safehouse had been compromised and the witness almost killed. Of course, that was why they should have brought in the marshals in the first place, but *nooooo . . .* the feebies thought they could handle it. *Not.*

Now with the guy securely ensconced in a new safehouse, guarded by a team of marshals from the Reno, Nevada headquarters, Quinn and Owens were arriving back in San Francisco eight hours after they'd left. They would have been back sooner but westbound I-80, just west of Sacramento, had been backed up for miles with the highway closed due to fatal accident involving three tractor trailers and two cars. As soon as Quinn had heard that on the radio, he'd changed their route so they could get around the mess. That, combined with the late hour and the curfews in effect, the roads were relatively quiet.

"You know, I'm still floored about the judges. That's some fucked-up shit they've got going on," Owens stated while yawning on the last word.

"You're telling me. I was gonna start asking for flashcards to keep all the players straight."

Owens grunted. "Hope they nail every one of those bastards. Fifteen! Do you fucking believe that? Fifteen fucking dirty judges. And those are the ones we know are going down. How many more crooked rats slipped through the cracks?"

"What the fuck?"

Quinn's question had Owens's gaze returning to the road ahead of them and repeating the same words. "What the fuck?"

The roadway leading onto the Bay Bridge had been blocked off by several military trucks and barricades. Members of the National Guard were rerouting the light traffic to an exit ramp, not allowing anyone to pass them and drive over the bridge. To go around would take forever. Flipping the headlights off, putting on the flashers, and pulling onto the left shoulder, Quinn slowly drove forward.

Owens retrieved his US Marshal shield and ID from his back pocket as Quinn did the same.

Several guards dressed in camo and holding their assault rifles went on alert when the vehicle approached. When they waved for Quinn to steer his car toward the exit, he slowed down even further, rolled down his window, and held his shield case out. One of the guards skimmed his flashlight beam over Quinn's outstretched hand, the light reflecting off the gold-toned metal. He then indicated for the vehicle to continue its approach.

Quinn stopped next to him and two other men. "Hey, guys. US Marshals. Quinn Alexander, and this is Bryan Owens. What's going on?"

The guard, with sergeant stripes on his sleeve and the name "Hamill" on his left chest pocket, glanced at the shields and IDs being held up for him to see. "Evening, sir. The bridge had to be shut down earlier. Rioters getting out of hand on the other end. Should be opening it up again in a bit, though. Where are you headed?"

"Potrero Hill," Owens said from where he was leaning over from the passenger seat. "What are the chances we can get a pass right now? I'm too fucking tired to take the hour detour around."

Quinn agreed. The residential section of the city where his partner lived with his family, not far from the trauma center where Carson worked, was only about fifteen to twenty minutes from where they were now. Quinn and Carson's condo was only another ten minutes further southwest from Potrero Hill in Bernal Heights. If they had to drive around, via the Golden Gate Bridge or San Mateo Bridge, it would easily take them an hour and a half to get to Owens's house. His wife had dropped him off at the office that morning because his truck's engine was being worked on. Quinn would take the SUV home and swap it out for his personal vehicle from the office parking lot tomorrow.

"Let me check with my boys on the other side with SFPD."

Hamill turned his head to the side and reached up to push the button on the speaker/mic on his shoulder, that was attached to the radio on his hip. But before he had a chance to say anything, static followed by shouts came over the airwaves. "Shots fired! Shots fired! West end of the bridge! I repeat, we're taking fire!"

"Shit!" Hamill and his men ran to their vehicles, loaded up, and took off across the bridge.

Quinn raised an eyebrow at Owens in an unspoken question. The other man nodded. "Go. I'll grab the vests."

Gunning the engine, Quinn drove up over the curb and around the heavy barricades as his partner reached into the backseat and retrieved the bulletproof vests they'd tossed back there earlier. Anytime they were escorting a witness, they wore them, but on the way home there had been no need for extra protection. As they crossed the span, the flashing lights from two SFPD cars, that they hadn't been able to see from the other end, bounced off the heavy girders of the bridge. The taillights from the military vehicles ahead of them brightened, and Quinn slammed on his brakes as well. With his window still down, they could hear rapid automatic gunfire coming from the other direction. *Shit. The bastards have freaking assault rifles.*

The eight guardsmen rolled out of their vehicles and used them for cover. Without radios, Quinn and Owens didn't know where the cops and soldiers, who'd been at the far end and called in the attack, currently were. All they could see were dozens of rioters, dressed mostly in black with their faces covered by bandanas, shooting at the new arrivals.

After parking behind one of the military trucks, Quinn took the vest Owens handed him and exited the vehicle. Keeping his body behind cover, he pulled on the protective Kevlar and drew his weapon. The Glock 22 was loaded with .40 caliber bullets—fifteen in the magazine, one in the chamber—and he had a spare magazine attached to his belt above his left, front pocket. Attached to his ankle was his backup weapon—a Glock 26 with ten 9mm rounds.

Keeping low, Quinn headed where Sgt. Hamill was yelling orders into his shoulder mic. Apparently, they couldn't return fire without risking hitting innocent people who were scattered all over the place on the far end of the span. From what Quinn could hear over the sergeant's radio, there were cops, soldiers, and civilians hit. Smoke grenades had been set off—by either the good guys or the bad guys—making it difficult to see the other end. It was uncertain if backup was on the way—someone on the military radio said moments before the gunfire started, the cops noticed their radios had gone silent. It was possible someone had taken out one of the transmission towers or it was just a coincidence since the system had glitches a few times a year. The city-wide EMS system had a backup in case of such emergencies, but it took several minutes for the frequencies to be switched over. Riots and gunfire were making a war zone out of different parts of the city. On the bridge, there were at least a dozen rabid gang members, firing on the military and police, and they were headed toward the fresh meat. Quinn ducked behind the truck when another volley of rounds went whizzing by. It was like being back in Desert Storm all over again, but this time, it was on US soil and the enemy was the country's own citizens.

"Fuck!"

Owens's curse over the rest of the din had Quinn's gaze seeking out his partner. The man was eyeing a young soldier who'd been hit in the shoulder and was lying on the ground, in the line of fire. Quinn realized what Owens was about to do, and he let out his own string of curses. Pivoting around the back of the truck, Quinn opened fire on the approaching attackers to give his partner a chance to get the injured man to safety. On either side of him, the other guardsmen did the same, but they were outnumbered. They limited their shots to several vehicles that were being driven slowly toward them, giving the mob something to hide behind.

Quinn prayed there were no innocents still in the line of fire as Owens reached the injured man and grabbed him under the armpits from behind. More shots rang out, and Quinn watched in horror as his partner's head snapped backward, stopping him short. A bullet ripped through him, exploding out the back of his skull. It was almost like a slow-motion scene in a movie as he dropped to his knees, before falling on top of the guard.

"Noooo!" Quinn didn't think twice. Staying low, he rushed over to his fallen partner. It didn't register right away that there was nothing that could be done for Owens, but when he reached the two men, it was obvious only one could be saved. With the firefight still raging, Quinn reluctantly rolled Owens off the guard, then dragged the injured man behind another truck. He'd mourn later. Right now, he still had to battle to save his own life and those of the men fighting beside him.

Two guardsmen joined Quinn, and he let one, who'd announced he was a medic, take over in tending to the injured man. The medic got his patient to his feet, and the two of them made their way behind Quinn's car, further away from the gunfire, while the other guard took position behind the truck with Quinn and launched several smoke grenades toward the approaching tangos.

Shit. Tangos. That was a word Quinn hadn't used in reference to the enemy since his Marine Corps days, but, right here and now, it fit. These weren't protesters—they were terrorists of the domestic kind. They didn't give a crap about anyone but themselves.

"We're clear to fire!" Hamill shouted from his position before rolling out and aiming his weapon at the closest black-clad person. He must have heard something over is radio that Quinn hadn't, but someone on the far end of the span must have said they could shoot without the risk of hitting an innocent on that side. Gunfire erupted from both sides once more. Several guards were ordered to again target the approaching vehicles, blowing out the tires to stop them in their tracks.

Doing a quick peek around the back of the truck, Quinn saw a male with an assault rifle emerging from behind a blue Honda through the gray smoke. Quinn brought his weapon up and fired. The bullet hit the suspect in the chest and spun him around before he dropped to the ground. That seemed to be the turning point. The rest of the tangos realized they were being fired upon and began to retreat while still shooting toward Quinn and the guardsmen. Another dark figure went down moments before Sgt. Hamill cursed. Quinn glanced over and saw the man had been hit in the upper arm, but it didn't appear to be slowing him down.

Flashing lights approached from behind them. An ambulance was coming toward them at a high rate of speed. The driver must have gone around the barriers, without question, since earlier the bridge had been open to emergency traffic only.

Another volley of gunfire had the men ducking behind their respective covers again, but a deafening blast came from behind as the front right tire of the ambulance was hit. It skidded out of control and headed straight for Quinn and the guard who was with him.

"Shit!" With nowhere else to go, Quinn grabbed the guardsman's vest and yanked him over the waist-high, cement barrier of the side of the bridge, before following him over. There was a narrow walkway for the Caltran workers who maintained the bridge, and then metal railings which Quinn and the guard landed against. But luck wasn't on their side as ambulance collided with the concrete. The 14,000-pound rig lifted off the ground and came over blockade striking the metal railing, ripping it apart at its joints with a sickening screech, and sending it plummeting to the water forty feet below. Quinn felt himself going over the side and tried grasping anything within reach that he could, but his hands only found thin air as the pull of gravity was too much. The weightlessness of his fall had his stomach bottoming. Thank God—not that he had time to—but his years of jumping out of airplanes in the Marines had his body reacting faster than his mind—which was good since his mind was shorting out. He flipped himself over so his feet would hit the water first, then tucked his arms tightly into his sides. He tilted his hips just enough to hit the water at an angle instead of straight in. Either way, it was going to hurt like hell, but the slanted position would hopefully keep him from breaking his legs upon impact. He took a deep breath and prepared for the worst.

Slamming into the frigid water was bone-jarring and knocked the air from his lungs. Quinn felt like he'd gotten hit by a Mac truck as he plunged into the darkness below the surface. The strong current of the San Francisco Bay, rushing out to meet the Pacific Ocean, sucked him further into the deep. His boots, vest, and clothing were putting him at a disadvantage as the murky water surrounded him and he fought to stay conscious. This wasn't how he wanted to die— not with so much he still wanted to do with his life . . . and with Carson.

CHAPTER FOURTEEN

With two anesthetists on his heels, Carson jogged down the stairs to the emergency room, rocking his head from side to side, trying to loosen the kinks there. After Quinn had called and told him it would be well after midnight when he got home, Carson had contacted Turk to see if his buddy wanted to go surfing for a few hours. As expected, the man had taken him up on the offer. They'd caught some decent waves, before the two of them grabbed something to eat at Turk's favorite sports bar. After dinner, Carson had gone home and crawled into bed earlier than usual, falling asleep after reading a dozen or so pages in the latest Brad Taylor novel.

He was thanking his lucky stars he'd gotten some sleep because all hell had broken loose in the city. His cell phone had rung a few hours after he'd dozed off —the hospital needed all hands on deck. There'd been multiple shootings, stabbings, and other incidents including a multi-vehicle accident caused by a terrified, female driver trying to get away from a few punks who'd attempted to carjack her, or worse, at a stop light. Carson had been in two surgeries already, and now he was heading to the ER after they'd reported more casualties were coming in. More than half his staff had arrived not long after receiving their own callouts, but he'd put the rest of the anesthesiologists and anesthetists on standby only. There would need to be change of shifts in a few hours, with well-rested doctors and nurse practitioners swapping out with the ones who'd been up most of the night.

Striding into the ER, Carson checked in with the head nurse who pointed to first trauma room, while she was on the phone asking for lab results. Two of the three cots in that room were occupied, with nurses, doctors, and technicians tending to the patients. Carson indicated for his team members to check on the casualties in the other two trauma rooms. From the sound of things, there'd been another shootout near the San Francisco Bay-Oakland Bridge, and the three critical-care rooms were already filled for the third time that night. That didn't include all the other cubicles throughout the large ER, which were occupied by a wide variety of medical emergencies and non-critical injuries. Entering Trauma #1, Carson took in the activity. It was clear one patient was somewhat stable, but the other was on the verge of going into traumatic arrest from the multiple bullets that had ripped through his body.

Moving to the head of the victim, Carson took over ventilating him with an ambu-bag and said to the nurse he'd relieved, "Pull over the intubation tray and prep a size 7 for me. Let me have a straight blade."

After connecting the requested metal blade to a handle, the nurse set it down on the cot next to the victim's head, as Carson forced air into the young man's mouth and nose. He hyperventilated the lungs, then grabbed the waiting instrument and a long, lubricated, plastic tube that was handed to him. With practiced precision, he opened the patient's mouth, eased the blade inside, with its tiny light illuminating the way, and used it to move the tongue out of the way. Crouching slightly to see into the man's throat, Carson threaded the tubing down into the trachea and stopped right above the carina which was where the airway was split into the two bronchi. If not done correctly, the tube could end up in the esophagus and then there would be no vital air getting into the victim's lungs.

The nurse removed the face mask from the ambu-bag and connected latter to the end of the tube sticking out of the man's mouth. She held the tube in place and squeezed the oxygen-filled bag while Carson put his stethoscope in his ears and listened to the patient's chest to make sure the tube was in the right place and filling the lungs.

Meanwhile, two paramedics rushed in with another loaded stretcher, and sirens, that could be heard in the distance through the open door leading to the ambulance bay, warned there were more coming in. The new patient was conscious, but his military fatigues were covered in blood from a shoulder wound, and Carson assumed he was one of the many National Guards who'd been brought to help regain control of the city.

The emergency room doctor muttered a curse before asking one of the medics, "How many more are we expecting?"

"Got me—probably a lot more." the guy answered as he undid the straps holding his patient to the stretcher. "All I know is it's a war zone out there. There's multiple casualties near and on the Bay Bridge. Civilians, National Guard, and at least two cops. Oh, and I heard two US Marshals were there too. One was shot in the head and DOA. The other went over the side into the bay from midspan with one of the guardsmen. It was either that or get crushed by an ambulance that lost control after the tires got shot out. The marine units are out searching for them."

With the chaos around him, it took a moment for the man's words to register in Carson's mind as he taped the patient's endotracheal tube in place, while a respiratory technician took over the ambulance-bag from the nurse. When the words did finally kick in, his hands froze as his head whipped up and his panicked gaze found the medic. "US Marshals? Who? What were their names? What did they look like?"

The medic shook his head as he helped transfer his patient onto the hospital gurney. "I don't know. I didn't even see them. One of the guys from the National Guard told me. We never made it actually onto the bridge—there were plenty of patients on the ramp leading up to it and a triage was set up."

Carson's heart threatened to beat out of his chest. Was Quinn the marshal who'd been shot and killed or was he the one who'd jumped God knew how many feet to the cold water below? Had he survived the jump? At this time of the night, what were the chances of another pair of marshals coming across the bridge heading in the direction to where both men lived.

The blood drained from his face as a million more questions flashed through his mind. A hand on his arm startled him. One of his anesthetists, Tina, had apparently come in and heard the exchange. "I've got this. Go call and find out what's going on. I hope it's not Quinn."

Numb, he stepped aside and let her take over. She would help the staff get the patient upstairs. Not even sure if he'd thanked her or not, Carson quickly left the room and ducked into the doctor's report room for some privacy. Yanking his cell phone from the pocket of his scrub pants, he checked to see if he'd missed any calls. Finding none, he held down the #2 button until it autodialed Quinn's cell. Carson's fear increased with each unanswered ring before the call went to voice mail. "Damn it!"

When the beep sounded, his words came out in a rush. "Quinn, babe, please call me as soon as you get this. I just heard . . . I . . . please, call me and let me know you're okay. If you can't get through, call the OR and tell them to get me." He swallowed a lump in his throat as his eyes welled up. "I love you."

After disconnecting the call, he thumbed through his contacts and found the direct line to Quinn's office. After three rings, a woman answered, "US Marshals, how can I help you?"

"Yes, I'm trying to get ahold of Deputy Quinn Alexander. Is he there?"

"Are you a witness, sir?"

"No, I'm his significant other, Carson Matthews." Quinn hadn't hidden the fact he was gay, and in a long-term relationship, from his new co-workers and bosses, and they didn't seem to have a problem with it. "I'm an anesthesiologist at SF General and heard there was a shooting on the Bay Bridge. I . . . I don't know if it's him."

He barely noticed the quiver in his voice, but the woman apparently had. Her tone softened. "I'm sorry, but I don't have any further information on that. This is just the switchboard for all the California Marshals' offices. All calls have been forwarded to us from the San Francisco office. My understanding is the supervisors and other deputies were heading to the scene."

"You can't tell me if it's Quinn or his partner, Bryan Owens?"

"I'm sorry. I haven't gotten word who's involved or their conditions."

"Can you find out? I . . . please, I have to know." Carson didn't know what he'd do if he had to sit and wait for a return call.

"I'm very sorry, but I can't. The best I can do is give your name and number to the supervisors when they check in."

He was ready to scream in frustration, but it wasn't this woman's fault. Hell, he didn't even know if she was answering his call here in San Francisco or some other city in the state. "All right. Please tell them to call me either way." He rattled off his cell phone number, then just in case, he also gave her the direct line to the OR.

Hanging up, Carson wracked his mind trying to think who could help him. Unfortunately, in the few months they'd been in San Francisco, he hadn't met any police officers except in passing. Back in San Diego, he knew quite a few of them just from the neighborhood he and Quinn had lived in.

"Dr. Matthews, please call the OR. Dr. Matthews, please call the OR."

Damn it. He picked up the landline phone on the desk and dialed the extension. One of the nurses answered. "OR."

"Amanda, it's Carson. What's up?"

"We've got three coming up from the ER, one

coming from the ICU, and maternity has an emergency C-section that can't take a spinal block. I've got no one to send."

Shit. Shit. Shit. "I'll send Tina to maternity, then I'll be up with one of the multi gunshots in a few minutes. Do me a favor—if Quinn or anyone from the marshals' office calls, let me know immediately."

"Everything okay?"

"I don't know. Just let me know if he calls."

"You got it."

Carson set the handset back on the phone's cradle, then headed back out to the chaotic ER. As much as he wanted to get into his car and drive to the bridge to find out what was going on, he had a job to do—one that required him to keep his head in the game. It was too early to call Turk, but if Carson didn't hear from Quinn by 6 a.m., his friend was getting a wake-up call. Turk had connections all over the place—Carson just prayed he wouldn't need to make that call.

QUINN WATCHED AS A COAST GUARD RESCUE swimmer dropped feet first into the water from the helicopter hovering overhead. He had no idea how long the current had been pulling him closer to the Pacific Ocean. It'd felt like hours but was probably only twenty or twenty-five minutes. He'd fought the unconsciousness that would have been his death

146

sentence, causing him to drown the watery tomb, and managed to break through the surface after struggling out of his bulletproof vest. His cell phone, that'd been on his hip, and his weapon had been lost somewhere between the fall and impact with the bay. Once he'd gulped as much fresh air as he could, his tactical shoes were the next to go. It hadn't been easy, but waterlogged, they'd made staying afloat more difficult. After the extra weight was gone, Quinn let his legs drift up and lead him in the direction of the current. The guardsmen who'd fallen off the bridge with him was nowhere to be seen. In the darkness, it was almost impossible to locate anything in the water.

By the time the spotlight from one of the three rescue helicopters had finally zeroed in on him, his arms and legs were painfully numb from the cold. Even though the night air was warm and comfortable, the water temperature around this time of the year was usually about fifty-five degrees. From what he could recall from his military training, at that temperature, he had one to two hours before exhaustion and hypothermia would do what the fall hadn't done—put him in an early grave. His teeth chattered, and a wave created from the helicopter's downdraft slapped him in the face, causing him to cough violently.

As the rescuer swam closer, he shouted over the thumping of the chopper blades. "Try to relax! Don't panic! I'll get you!"

Quinn knew the routine. Another thing he'd trained for in the Marines. Many times, when someone is in a near-drowning situation, they become frantic and, in their quest, to stay afloat, they start thrashing around, hitting the very person trying to save them. He gave the guy a shaky thumbs-up and allowed the rescuer to grab him from behind. The man's arm wrapped around Quinn's chest, supporting him.

"Are you injured!"

"D-Don't think s-so! Banged up b-but nothing m-major!"

"Hang tight! Gonna get you in the basket and lift you out of here!"

Within minutes, Quinn was being pulled onboard the helicopter, which hovered over the bay until they retrieved the rescuer. While they were hauling the guy up, an Aviation Survival Technician (AST) covered Quinn with blankets to keep up warm. "We heard two of you went over! Did you see the other guy down there at all?"

Quinn shook his head as his body trembled uncontrollably. "N-Never saw him come up! I was almost knocked out! N-Not s-sure how long I was in there before I remembered what'd happened and that I wasn't the only one!"

"We'll have the other two choppers keep looking while we get you to the hospital!" He placed an oxygen mask over Quinn's face then proceeded to check for injuries. While he was sore and cold as hell,

Quinn didn't think he broke anything which shocked the hell out of him. It wasn't as if he'd never jumped from that height into a body of water before, but it'd been years, and he'd been prepared for it every time.

Once the rescue swimmer was on board, the helicopter banked to the west. They landed in an empty parking lot near one of the marinas where the fire department had set up a landing zone and an ambulance was waiting for him. The EMTs got him settled on the stretcher and loaded him up. Before they pulled out of the lot, Quinn addressed the man in the back with him. "Can you take me to SF General? I've got family working there."

"That's where we're headed. No problem."

Now that he wasn't in danger of dying, Quinn's thoughts drifted to Owens and wondered if their supervisors had been notified and who was going to have to knock on the man's home to tell his family. Quinn still couldn't wrap his brain around the fact his partner was dead. As soon as they reached the hospital, he'd contact Carson and let him know what happened. *Jeez, he's going to flip the fuck out.*

CHAPTER FIFTEEN

"How're his vitals, Carson?"

He glanced at the monitor, then back at Dr. Lillian Coats who was performing the surgery on the gunshot victim. "Eighty over forty; pulse 110."

"Damn. All right, let's hang another unit of blood. It's going to take a while to repair the damage. Might have to take the spleen."

Which meant they were going to be in the OR for at least another hour. For the third time in five minutes, Carson checked the clock on the wall of the surgery suite. He'd left word at the desk for them to let him know if Quinn called, but over almost two hours later, no one had used the intercom or come in to tell him anything. How he was concentrating on the patient he had no idea.

Quinn couldn't be dead. Carson thought for sure he'd feel it in his gut if the love of his life was gone. His grandmother had known when his grandfather had died before she'd even heard he'd collapsed while golfing. No one could ever explain how, but when the phone rang, she'd asked Carson's dad to answer it because it was bad news.

Maybe the reason Quinn hadn't called was he was running around dealing with the investigation into the death of at least one marshal. Maybe it was because of the riots . . . or he was still out of the city completely on the callout from hours earlier. *God, please let him be on his way home from somewhere else.*

As he cocked his head from side to side, trying to work out the kinks in his neck, the door to the scrub room opened. One of the other anesthesiologists strode in, freshly scrubbed. Even though she was wearing a mask on her face and her hair up under a cap, he knew it was Patty Greene. His eyes narrowed as she approached and held out her hand for the clipboard he was holding. "I'll take over. Quinn's down in the ER asking for you; he's alert and stable—that's all I know."

"Oh, thank God." The relief coursing through him rendered him immobile for a moment, but Patty's hand on his shoulder prompted him to stand and let her have the chair behind the patient's head. He didn't need to give her a status update since all the information was on the chart she took from him. "Thanks, Patty."

"No problem. Just remember this next time you're making a holiday rotation schedule."

He grinned behind his mask as he started for the door. "You got it."

After ripping off his mask and cap and tossing them in the laundry basket, he hurried out to the elevators. As usual, they were on the upper floors and there was no way he was waiting for them. He still didn't know if Quinn was badly hurt or if he was hurt at all. Carson wouldn't completely relax until he laid on eyes on his lover and assured himself he was okay.

The ER was still hopping; at this point he didn't think it would ever slow down. Instead of checking each room and cubicle until he found Quinn, he checked the charts at the nurses' station. When he spotted "Alexander, Quinn" assigned to a general, patient-assessment cubicle, he breathed a little easier —if Quinn had been hurt badly, he would have been on the other side of the emergency room where critical and semi-critical patients were treated. It still didn't stop Carson from rushing over. Yanking the curtain back, he took in the scene.

Quinn was lying on a gurney, talking to one of his supervisors—Carson couldn't remember her name at the moment, and didn't even acknowledge her. He was too busy assessing the man he loved for injuries. Several heavy blankets had been piled on top of Quinn, and his hair was still damp. He was hooked up to monitors and IV tubing ran from a bag hanging on a hook, then snaked under the blankets where it had been inserted in either his hand or his arm. He was pale, and his lips tinged blue, but his eyes were alert as he turned to Carson. "Hey."

"Hey? Hey? That's all you can say? Did you . . . I— I heard what happened on the bridge almost two hours ago . . ." A lump forming in his throat prevented him from saying anything more.

"Shit." Quinn glanced at his supervisor. "Can you give us a few minutes?"

With a sympathetic expression on her face, she nodded. "Sure. Let me go touch base with everyone. I'll be back in a few."

The dark-haired, woman in her mid-forties gave Carson a small smile as she skirted around the curtain, then closed it behind her. Quinn uncovered one arm and held it out. Grasping it, Carson closed the distance between them. Quinn's skin was cold to the touch, and Carson tucked both their hands back under the blanket, refusing to let go. "That—that was you? Who jumped off the bridge?"

"Well, I didn't exactly jump, but, yeah, that was me." Sadness filled his eyes, and Carson knew what he was about to say next. "Owens was shot and killed. He was pulling a guy from the National Guard to safety and . . ."

Apparently, Carson wasn't the only one with a lump in his throat. Dragging over a metal and plastic chair, he sat in it while glancing at the monitor over Quinn's head that gave his blood pressure, EKG, and oxygen saturation. His vitals were stable, thank God.

Carson leaned forward a brushed a gentle kiss over his lover's lips. "I—I thought I lost you."

One corner of Quinn's mouth ticked upward in a sad smile. "Can't get rid of me that easily, babe. I'm so sorry I worried you. How'd you hear about it?"

"From the paramedics who'd brought in some of the victims from the shootout. All he knew was a marshal had been shot and killed and another had fallen off the bridge after almost getting crushed by an ambulance. Is that what happened?"

He nodded. "Yeah. It's sort of a long story, and I'm really not up to telling it again—I've already told it three times to the cops and my supervisor—but I'll tell you about it later, okay?"

"Yeah. That's fine." Carson wasn't upset about that at all—he had a feeling he would need the extra time to compose himself in order to hear all the gory details. "So, I guess I'm adding a shrink to the list of doctors you need." He'd said it in a wry manner, but it was true. Quinn was going to need a professional to deal with everything that'd happened earlier whether he was willing to admit it or not.

Quinn snorted as his eyelids drooped. "Yeah, sure. Add it to the list."

Carson caressed Quinn's wrist with his thumb. "Close your eyes and rest. I'll be here when you wake up again—I promise."

Surprisingly, he did as instructed, before squeezing Carson's hand three times. He didn't open his eyes again as he spoke. "I love you, babe.

Thinking of you was what helped me survive out there, waiting to be rescued. I knew I had to get back to you."

It was obvious exhaustion was overtaking Quinn. Carson reached up with his unoccupied hand and brushed a lock of the Dom's hair back off his forehead. "Thank you for making it. I love you too. Now rest."

Quinn was sound asleep within minutes, and Carson kept his promise and stayed with him. He could have lost the love of his life tonight, but somehow, the gods of fate had made sure that didn't happen, and Carson would be forever grateful.

HOURS LATER, CARSON GLANCED AT THE SCREEN OF his vibrating phone and sighed. He'd meant to call Danilo back earlier, but had forgotten his cousin had called—probably to talk about his hot date last night with Master Hisoka. The two of them had hit it off big time. Carson couldn't remember the last time his younger cousin had been so excited about a Dom he was seeing. Usually there was something lacking in the relationship, either on the boyfriend side or the Dom side. It was about time Danilo had found someone who was comfortable and strong enough to be a combination of both.

After stabbing the connect button, he then brought the phone to his ear. "Hey."

"Never mind 'hey!'" Danilo shouted over the line, startling Carson. "I've been trying to call you all night and all this morning! I must have left you like a zillion messages. Quinn too!"

"Sorry, cuz. I was in surgery. I saw the messages when I took a break, but thought you were just calling to tell me about your date. All hell was breaking loose here and then I had to deal with Quinn in the ER."

Danilo's tone dropped in confusion. "Deal with Quinn? Oh, shit! I heard what happened on the bridge. That wasn't—"

"Yeah, it was." He closed his eyes as the horrors of the last few hours came rushing back. "He's okay—as okay as someone can be after falling off a fucking bridge. And it was his partner that was shot and killed."

"Jesus. Is he hurt bad?"

"Banged up pretty good, but he didn't break anything—don't ask me how. Half training, half luck as he tells it. He's not even here—he signed himself out of the ER and went back to the office to give his statement. I'll be so glad when he puts his resignation in. He's not the only one stressed out about his job. I've got a few white hairs from this, let me tell you." Not wanting to dwell on how different things could've turned out over the past twenty-four hours, Carson changed the subject. "So, how'd your date go?"

"About as good as your night did."

There was a pause, then Danilo let shaky breath. It sounded like he was crying. *What the fuck?*

"Hisoka's ex-Dom, Jeff, has apparently been stalking him. He jumped us outside the cafe, beat the holy hell out of Hisoka, and locked me up on his boat. He left me all tied up and took Hisoka off somewhere else in his car."

"What the fuck? Are you okay?" *Holy shit! What else could go wrong in such a short amount of time?*

"I guess. I mean, physically, yes, but the cops—when the guy on the next boat got security to come let me out and call the cops, they thought we'd had a three way that went bad. That Hisoka and Jeff left me there on purpose to go somewhere by themselves. I tried to get them to call Quinn. They wouldn't listen until one of the paramedics mentioned she knew Hisoka and he wasn't like that. Then they agreed to call the security desk in his building to see if they'd gone there. They ended up talking to Turk somehow, and he told them he'd been expecting Hisoka back to pick up the dogs and he hadn't shown up yet. The building security told the cops that, yes, they had a note on file about the stalker."

Anger started to rise within Carson. "He knew he had a stalker, and he didn't fucking say anything to you?"

"The guy lives in San Diego. Hisoka and his brother filed a complaint and that seemed to be the end of it after he moved up here. He never ran into him again. He didn't even think Jeff knew where he lived."

"Until last night."

"Yeah."

Carson pinched the bridge of his nose and tried to calm down. "Okay, then. So, he didn't expose you to a nut job on purpose. Wait. Where are you now? Do they know where Hisoka is? Is he okay?"

"No! He's gone, and I'm home worried shitless. That's what I've been trying to tell you. This guy has completely lost it. He was talking about punishing his sub for leaving him and all sorts of stuff. He was punching him in the face, knocked him clean out, Carson." Danilo's voice broke off with a sob.

"Jesus Christ. I'm so sorry. I can try to call Quinn, but he told me he might not be able to answer the phone while rehashing everything that happened for his supervisors. And they're getting him a new phone since his is at the bottom of the bay. I'll let him know as soon as I can, okay? Maybe he can make sure everything is being handled properly. In the meantime, stay positive. Hisoka is going to really need you after this. I'll stop by later and check on you, okay? I'm stuck at the hospital for a few more hours. Call me if you hear anything—anything at all. I swear I'll answer this time. And lock your doors. This guy may have followed him to your place."

"Okay. I will. And tell Quinn to be more careful. He's not an action hero."

Carson snorted. "Yeah, he's not, but I doubt

that'll stop him from trying to save the world." He paused, not ready to hang up yet. He was worried about Danilo. Just when the younger man had found someone he was really into, things had gone to shit. "Have you eaten?"

"No, I'm not hungry."

"You've got to eat something—I don't care how small. You need your strength. Promise me."

Danilo sniffled. "Yeah, I promise."

"Good. I'll talk to you later. Call me if you need me."

"I will. Later."

Carson disconnected the call and blew out a ragged breath. He didn't know how much more he could take before he ran up to the hospital roof and screamed his lungs out.

CHAPTER SIXTEEN

After being dismissed by his supervisors and the IAB deputies, Quinn let out a long, deep breath then pushed his chair away from the conference table, then stood and left the room. The door closed behind him, and now all he could do was wait. It was standard procedure for Internal Affairs to investigate any line of duty death. They'd arrived just as Quinn had returned to the office with his fellow deputies and Supervisory Deputy Muldoon, after stopping by Owens's house to see his widow and children who'd already been notified of his death.

When Monica Owens had seen Quinn walk into her home, she'd caught him off guard and thrown herself into his arms, sobbing. While he'd only been partnered with the man for less than a year, Quinn had gotten to know his family over the occasional barbecues and other events. Holding Monica's trembling body, he'd been unable to prevent finally breaking down and crying for the loss of the man who'd become a good friend. Before Quinn and his SD left, they made arrangements for the Owens family to have at least one of the deputies at the house all day to help with everything that went with planning a funeral. It was a given that hundreds of members of law enforcement would most likely be attending, and because of that, it took quite a bit of organizing.

Carson had been a little pissed Quinn had checked himself out of the ER after the doctors confirmed he hadn't broken anything, but there had been no reason for him to stay. The Tylenol they'd given him wasn't doing much for the pain from the bruises covering much of his body, but that was nothing compared to the other injuries and deaths that had occurred on that bridge. Six hours after the fall, the body of the missing soldier from the National Guard had finally been found in the bay, two miles south of the bridge. Last Quinn had heard, several others had lost their lives up on the bridge, with many more injured.

The conference room door swung open and the three-man IAB team strode out and headed for the exit without even glancing in Quinn's direction. Muldoon called him back in. Once he was inside, she closed the door again and took a seat across the table from him. "They're going to follow up with the ambulance crew and the guards, but you'll most likely be cleared without a problem."

Looking up at the ceiling, Quinn breathed a sigh of relief. One of the IAB deputies, who clearly had a Napoleon complex—at five feet five, he seemed to overcompensate for his short stature by being an overly-aggressive to make himself feel important—had been harping on the fact Quinn had followed the guardsmen onto the bridge. It was that decision—according to the little shit—that had gotten Owens killed. Quinn had stressed he hadn't made the decision alone—not that he was blaming his partner. Neither one of them could, in good conscience, have left the soldiers to fend for themselves. None of the deputies they worked with would have done anything different, having already voiced that to Quinn when he'd been second guessing everything while lying on the hospital gurney.

"Quinn." Her tone had softened and when his gaze met hers, she continued. "I know everyone else in the office told you this, but now it's my turn. If I was at the barricade when that shit went down, I would have done exactly what you'd done. We run in when everyone else is running away. We put our lives on the line every damn day and pray we'll make it home to our families. It's the way we're wired. But we also know that if we don't make it home, our loved ones will always have the support of the others in this office. Always. I'm sorry about Bryan—he was a good man and had worked for me for several years. He'll be sorely missed, but don't you think for one single second that anyone in this office blames you for what happened up there. You were thrown into a situation most deputies would never see during their career unless they'd spent time in the military."

He swallowed the lump in his throat and nodded. "Thanks."

"None needed." She stood and stepped toward the door. "Why don't you head home and get some rest? You'll need to meet with the shrink tomorrow. I'll find out which one they're assigning you and call you later."

Quinn was about to thank her again, but his new, agency-issued phone rang. One of the other deputies had left it on his desk, after hooking it up to his cell number, to replace the one that was now at the bottom of the bay. Glancing at the number, he stabbed the connect button as Muldoon opened the door and returned to her office.

"Alexander."

"It's Mac. You okay?"

It was evident the detective had heard what had happened, even though he was still in the hospital recovering from his own near-death experience. "I think I'm one big bruise, but I'm alive. Wish I could say the same about my partner."

"I'm sorry. He was a good guy."

"Yeah, he was. Listen, I'm—" He'd been about to say he was going home and would talk to the man later, but Mac interrupted him.

"Quinn, I know it's a bad time, but I need really need your help."

He almost said, "whatever it is, I can't do it right now," but there was something in the other man's tone that, instead, had him saying, "What's up?"

"I know where Nicole Brown is."

"What? Where? Is she alive?"

"Yeah. But we need a team to go in and get her if she's going to stay that way. I can't tell you how I found out, but she's being held in some mansion in Clarendon Heights." He rattled off the address, and Quinn grabbed a nearby pen and pad and jotted the information down. "With the riots and shakedowns, the PD sources are limited. When you factor in who we can and can't trust, that number drops dramatically. What are the chances your SRT can respond and get her out?" The US Marshals' Special Response Team was the equivalent of the police department's SWAT.

Standing, he strode to the door with the phone still to his ear. "Hang on. Let me get my SD in on this. Since she'll probably need witness protection during the investigation into her father's crimes and how they're related to her kidnapping, we should be able to handle it."

Forty minutes later, Quinn was riding shotgun in the SUV driven by Muldoon. He'd changed from the scrubs and slippers Carson had procured for him at the ER into a clean pair of jeans, a T-shirt, and sneakers he kept in his truck for emergencies. He'd also grabbed a spare vest and weapon from the deputy in charge of the office's equipment room and armory. The SRT had been called out and search warrants had been obtained through Judge Fox. Quinn and Mac had both agreed Fox would be the best one to call for the warrants since he was already aware of their suspicions regarding Ms. Brown's disappearance.

Muldoon pulled into a commuter parking lot several blocks away from the target home and parked next to the SRT communications van with the US Marshal shield on the side. This would be moved to a closer location when they were ready to stage the rescue, but it wouldn't be able to be seen from the residence. Several unmarked vehicles were scattered around. While Muldoon jumped out without hesitation, Quinn groaned as every muscle in his body protested that he wasn't home in bed as he climbed out of the passenger seat. He'd wanted to be here since Mac couldn't be. The only way Muldoon had agreed to it was if Quinn stayed in the background. He was here as an observer, nothing more, since he was on administrative leave until the results of the IAB investigation were filed.

The head of SRT, Supervisory Deputy Mark Palmer shook Quinn's hand when he joined the group gathered at the back of the van. "Sorry to hear about Owens—he was a great guy."

"Thanks." Quinn didn't want his grief to wash over him again—not here—so he quickly changed the subject. "What have you got so far?"

Palmer pointed to blueprints that were spread out

on a folding table. "Corner house, front facing the side street. Driveway dumps out there too. Three-six hundred square feet. Three floors, four bedrooms, enclosed patio and a porch off the second floor. We'll have a team access the back from two houses down. The property is on a cliff, so no one will try to escape that way, but there's enough room for my guys to be able to come over the wall back there. We'll have another team entering here at the garage and the third team taking the front door. The house to the west is empty and for sale, so I've got two men in there now with eyes on the target house, but their sight line is limited. They've got an amplifier pointed at it but, so far, they haven't heard anything that indicates there's anyone in there, but that doesn't mean anything. It just means it's all quiet, and I hope it stays that way. Is there anything else we need to know before we get set for the breach?"

"Yeah," Quinn said. "It's possible the victim is DOA or she's been left there alive by herself. The detective who'd gotten the tip thinks there's a good chance the kidnappers no longer need her with the chief's death. If she never saw their faces, she may still be alive."

"Good to know, but we'll still go on the assumption there's tangos still on site. Anything else?"

"Not that I can think of."

Palmer clapped his hands once, garnering everyone's attention. "All right! Let's load up! And nobody get fucking hurt. With the riots, EMS is on overload and didn't have any buses to send for standby."

It took SRT ten minutes to report "all clear" and the victim was alive and in stable condition, after they'd breached the entrances to the multi-million-dollar home and searched the interior. Quinn, Muldoon, and several other deputies, who hadn't been involved in the initial breach and search, waited on the sidewalk at the end of the drive. Not far from where they stood, barricades had been set up to keep traffic from coming down the side street.

It wasn't much longer before Palmer and another SRT member escorted Nicole Brown from the house. Quinn was surprised to see her in relatively good condition. She was clean, with no visible injuries, and fully clothed under a throw blanket that was wrapped around her shoulders.

As they were deciding which vehicle to use to take her to the hospital for an evaluation, a Hummer approached the barricades and stopped short. A woman in a city EMS uniform jumped from the back seat and rushed over to the uniformed officer at the barricade. Quinn watched as she said something to the cop, who then turned to the activity behind him. "Deputy Palmer! Jen's a paramedic and can take a look at the lady for you." The cop was smart and hadn't called Nicole by her name or by "victim" or "hostage" since there were a few bystanders who'd come out of their houses to see what the commotion was all about.

Palmer's eyebrows shot up then he waved the woman over. She quickly ducked under the barricade and hurried over to where they stood. Quinn strode over, having recognized the woman, although he couldn't remember from where. Glancing back at the barricade, he saw the cop was preventing a man from passing. The man looked annoyed but didn't argue. He continued to talk with the officer, but his eyes remained on the female medic as she questioned her new patient about injuries and medical issues.

Quinn noticed the EMT's name badge. *Jen Galloway—Paramedic*. That name definitely rang a bell but he was still in the dark about where he'd met her before, not that it really mattered.

After determining Nicole was stable, Jen turned to Palmer and Quinn. "I know it'll take a while for you to get an ambulance here with all hell breaking loose, so, if you want, we can take her to the hospital —we're on our way there now."

The two men looked at each other, and Quinn got the impression the SRT's supervisor was thinking exactly what he was—Nicole would probably be better with another female until they got a better understanding of what she'd gone through. When Palmer gave him a nod, Quinn said, "That's fine. We appreciate it. I'll have two deputies in two vehicles escort you just to be on the safe side."

"That'd be great." She smiled at Nicole. "Come

on. Let's get you checked out. Is there anyone you want to call to meet you at the hospital?"

As the two women walked toward the barricade and the Hummer beyond, Quinn filled in Muldoon who had just gotten off her cell phone and joined them. She assigned deputies to lead and follow the Hummer, then address Palmer. "What did you find?"

He leaned against his vehicle, crossed his arms, and shook his head. "Weirdest freaking thing. Like your detective buddy suspected, Quinn, whomever had been holding Ms. Brown hostage left without a trace. She'd been in locked in a furnished bedroom with an attached bath. The room faced the rear of the house and the windows had been covered with plywood bolted to the frames. They did let her watch TV, though, and three times a day, she'd received a tray of food from a man wearing a mask. She's got no idea who he was or why she'd been kidnapped. She also doesn't have any idea why she was left there to be rescued. This morning was the first time no one brought her something to eat and around 1:00 this morning was the last time she'd heard anyone talking or walking around the house. All in all, she'd been treated very well, despite being held against her will. She says she wasn't assaulted in any way, just threatened she'd be hurt if she tried to escape or didn't comply with their orders. Unfortunately, with the TV available to her, she'd already learned of her father's death on the news."

"After she's checked out at the ER," Muldoon

said, "she'll be interviewed to see if she can give us anything to help get an arrest out of this, but it's sounding like she won't have much to tell. We'll get a crime scene unit in here to check for prints and other trace evidence."

"I doubt they'll find much. From the smell, someone used a lot of bleach and lemon-scented furniture polish recently. Probably to wipe the place clean."

It was sounding more and more like this was a professional job, and organized crime popped into Quinn's head. He was torn between asking Mac what the hell was going on and not wanting to know anything at all. Speaking of which, Quinn pulled his cell phone out and redialed the number the detective had called from earlier.

"Yeah?"

"It's Quinn. Target is safe and sound. She was left alone late last night and well taken care of these past few weeks."

"Glad to hear it."

Quinn bit his tongue. He'd decided he didn't want to know the details of how Mac had learned where the woman was being held. "I'm going to leave this for everyone else to wrap up and head home. It's going to be a rough few days."

"Yeah, I'm sure. Again, I'm sorry about Owens."

"Thanks. Take care of yourself and tell Harper I said hello."

"You got it" Mac paused, then added, "And Quinn?"

"Yeah?"

"I owe you big time . . . for a lot of things. You need me, just call."

"No offense, but I hope I never do. Take care."

Quinn disconnected the call and waited as Muldoon issued a few more orders before she turned to him. "You look exhausted. I'll drop you off at your place—you can get your truck tomorrow. I'll have someone drive it over to you if you need it before then."

"Tomorrow's good. It won't be long before Carson's home." The weight of the last few days was heavy on his shoulders. While he was, indeed, exhausted as Muldoon had said he looked, he doubted his sleep would be restful—at least, not for a while.

Following his SD down the driveway to where her vehicle was parked in the street, a shiver coursed through him as he passed the still idling ambulance. He didn't think he'd ever be able to see another one without reliving those moments of sheer terror as the one on the bridge barreled toward him, then sent him down into the water below. Once more, he thanked God for giving him more time on this Earth and wished the same courtesy had been afforded to Owens.

CHAPTER SEVENTEEN

S tanding stoically at the gravesite, Quinn pushed his sunglasses back up onto the bridge of his nose as the preacher blessed the flag-covered coffin that held the body of US Marshal Bryan Owens. Quinn's hand was on the shoulder of his deceased partner's wife as she and her two children sat in chairs in front of him, just to the left of the grave. They were flanked by her parents, siblings, and in-laws, all with tears rolling down their cheeks. Carson, who'd taken the day off work to be with him, stood to Quinn's right while his supervisors were to his left. There were over four hundred people attending the graveside service following the funeral at the family's church. Most of the mourners were members of law enforcement on the federal, state, and local levels. Marshals from all over had either driven or flown in to help bury one of their own.

This wasn't the only memorial many of them were

attending this week. Five San Francisco cops had been killed over the past nine days—two of whom Reid had personally killed. Needless to say, Reid, Mac, and Quinn hadn't gone to their funerals. As for disgraced Chief of Police Tom Brown, his family had had him cremated and buried in a very private service after the press had a field day with the corruption story. Sadly, six National Guardsmen and seven civilians had also lost their lives in the riots.

After the deaths and destruction that had taken place the night Owens was killed, the family of Holly Springs, the little girl whose tragic murder seemed to have sparked the mayhem, had gone on TV, with several civic leaders and clergymen, pleading with the public to settle down and end the riots. It appeared to have worked, as the last two nights had been relatively quiet in the city. Carson's surgical team had managed to sleep through both nights without a single callout. It had probably helped, in an ironic way, that the press had found a ripe story to chase and the riots had become old news.

The city-wide justice system had taken major hits this week, as well, as D.A. Graham Cartwright and fifteen judges, past and present, were arrested and facing indictments on a variety of charges, most of which were felonies. Instead of facing the music, one judge had committed suicide—ironically jumping off the same bridge Quinn had fallen from and survived. The major difference between the two was the judge had hit the water face first.

Quinn had spoken to Mac and Harper and was glad to hear they were doing well. Both the detective and Reid had been cleared of any wrongdoing in the shooting deaths of the chief and the other two officers, and Harper no longer needed to hide from her past. Quinn didn't want to know the full details, but he was happy she had a brighter future with the man she had clearly fallen in love with.

Danilo and Hisoka were also recovering from their own crisis. It was good to know they'd be there for each other as they healed. Quinn and Carson suspected a long-term contract was in the Dom and sub's future.

Crack! The first volley of shots for the twenty-one-gun salute startled Quinn back to the present, his heart rate spiking. Had it not been for Carson grasping his arm, evidently noticing his reaction, Quinn might have bolted. He managed to take a deep breath and let it out slowly as a second then third volley was fired. Turning his head slightly, he gave Carson a nod of thanks. Once again, Quinn was reminded his sub was there for him as much as the Dom was there for Carson. The give and take of their power exchange benefitted both in more ways than one, and Quinn knew it didn't mean he was weak when he needed to lean on his submissive instead of the other way around. Carson had already set up appointments for Quinn to see a PTSD psychologist first thing tomorrow morning, after deciding the one the Marshals had suggested didn't have a good reputation in the health-care community.

As "Taps" was played by a lone bugler, Quinn gently squeezed the widow's shoulder in support. She'd told him she didn't blame him for what had happened to her husband, and while a part of him was grateful, he would always wonder what he could have done differently that would have changed the outcome of that awful night. He knew, now more than ever, it was time to leave the Marshals. He had a face-to-face interview scheduled with Ian and Devon Sawyer, when they flew into San Francisco next week, but from what Jake had told Quinn, it was just a formality. The owners of Trident Security had apparently been impressed with his resumé and training and planned on offering him the job to run their satellite office in the city. They would also be interviewing several potential employees who would be working under Quinn and would allow him to sit in on the meetings and have a say in who was hired.

He hadn't said anything about his resignation to anyone at work yet, but he didn't think his supervisors were going to be surprised when he told them, especially after everything that had happened recently. With his caseload, he would have to arrange the transfer of his witness to other deputies—it would take several weeks to accomplish that—so he'd have to tell the Sawyers that he'd need about a month and a half before he could start with them.

Carson had been thrilled to hear Quinn was

retiring from the federal agency. What the submissive didn't know was Quinn had decided, since he was already making one huge change in his life, it was time to make another as well. He hadn't thought out the details yet, but at some point, in the next few weeks, he planned on proposing to Carson—something that was long overdue. Quinn couldn't imagine his life without his lover in it, nor did he want to.

As the services came to a close, SD Muldoon invited everyone to a local American Legion hall for a repast with the family and friends of Deputy Owens. Then one by one, the mourners stepped forward to lay a flower on the casket before heading back to their cars. Carson stood by Quinn's side as he paused for a moment to silently say goodbye to his partner and friend, then walked with him to his truck. Quinn didn't say a word when his sub gestured for him to take the passenger seat, before climbing in the driver's side. Instead of starting the vehicle, Carson turned to face Quinn. "Stupid question, I'm sure, but are you okay?"

Grasping the other man's hand, Quinn shook his head. "Not really. But I will be as long as you're with me. I'll probably need you to point out when I'm being an ass or keeping stuff in over the next few weeks, but that's what makes our relationship work—being there for each other. I love you, babe. I'm not sure how I would've made it through this week without you."

"I love you too, and I'm glad I could be here for you." Carson gave him a small smile. "If you're acting like an ass, can I threaten to flog you without getting in trouble?"

Quinn threw back his head and laughed for the first time in days. "Yeah, that'll never happen."

THE COLLECTIVE SEASON TWO NOVELS

Eight Standalone Novels: One Epic Crossover Event

If you missed out on any of The Collective Season Two books, or want to read the entire series again, follow the links below to grab your copies of these amazing books!

Featured authors in order of appearance-

Absolution—B.R. Bradley

Ensnared—Leona Windwalker

Gravity—J.L. Leslie

Swayed—Erin Trejo

Flawed—Jade Royal

Trust—Riley Edwards

Angst—Samantha A. Cole

Redemption—Ellie Masters

The Collective Website

The Collective Facebook Page

The Collective Newsletter

ACKNOWLEDGMENTS

To my fellow authors who invited me to be part of
this fun and amazing project. I had a blast!

ABOUT THE AUTHOR

USA Today Bestselling Author and Award-Winning Author Samantha A. Cole is a retired police officer and paramedic. She's lived her entire life in the suburbs of New York City and is looking forward to becoming a snow-bird between New York and Florida someday. Her two fur-babies, Jinx and Bella, keep her company and remind their mom to take a break from writing every once in a while to go for a walk, which is the best way to deal with a stubborn case of writer's block.

An avid reader since childhood, Samantha was often found with a book in hand and sometimes one in each. After being gifted with a stack of romance novels from her grandmother, her love affair with the genre began in her teens. Many years later, she discovered her love for writing stories was just as strong. Using her life experiences and training, she strives to find the perfect mix of suspense and romance for her readers to enjoy.

Her standalone novel, The Friar, won the silver medal in the 2017 Readers' Favorite Awards in the Contemporary Romance genre out of more than 1000 entries.

While the original planned stories for the Trident Security series have been completed, they have brought many opportunities for Samantha to spread her wings and bring her readers more characters and stories to love. Look for the Trident Security Omega Team series, the Doms of The Covenant Novella series, the new Hazard Falls series the upcoming Blackhawk Security series, and more from the Malone Brothers series, in addition to several standalone projects.

Join the Sexy Six-Pack's Sirens Group on Facebook
www.samanthacoleauthor.com

Website: www.samanthacoleauthor.com

facebook.com/SamanthaColeAuthor

twitter.com/SamanthaCole222

instagram.com/samanthacoleauthor

bookbub.com/profile/samantha-a-cole

goodreads.com/SamanthaCole

pinterest.com/samanthacoleaut

Made in the USA
Columbia, SC
10 October 2021

46542433R10119